"Still time to get out of here alive," Dustin panted, circling, looking for one last opening.

"Bastid!" Halverson screamed, feigning a thrust in the desperate hope that Dustin would commit himself and lose his balance.

Dustin's blade came down at the same instant, and it scored first. The two biggest fingers of Halverson's left hand were cleanly severed, and even before the scream could escape the bronc buster's mouth, Dustin whipped his blade in a backhand motion across the man's throat, opening it wide . . .

→◆→ WESLEY ELLIS ◆←◆─

LONE STAR

AND THE
TEXAS TORNADO

J

JOVE BOOKS, NEW YORK

LONE STAR AND THE TEXAS TORNADO

A Jove Book / published by arrangement with
the author

PRINTING HISTORY
Jove edition / December 1994

ISBN: 0-515-11506-1

A JOVE BOOK®
Jove Books are published by The Berkley Publishing Group,
200 Madison Avenue, New York, New York 10016.
JOVE and the "J" design are trademarks
belonging to Jove Publications, Inc.

PRINTED IN THE UNITED STATES OF AMERICA

10 9 8 7 6 5 4 3 2 1

LONE STAR

AND THE
TEXAS TORNADO

Chapter 1

Jessica Starbuck stepped outside her ranch house and filled her lungs with the sweet scent of Texas sage. She was long-legged with full breasts and a tawny mane of honey-blond hair that glinted in the sun like polished copper. Her green eyes missed very little as she studied her huge Circle Star Ranch, its seemingly endless vistas grazed by her thousands of Texas longhorn cattle.

Overhead, the sky was a deep indigo blue, and cloudless just as far as Jessie could see. The world seemed ripe with the promise of another good year. They'd had a mild winter and good spring rains so that the range was deep in grass and ablaze with wildflowers. Jessie knew that, in another month, it would be time to start her spring roundup. Since her ranch covered several thousand acres, it was going to be a big job, as usual, but it was one that she and her Circle Star ranch hands always anticipated.

Her tall, rangy foreman, Ed Wright, came riding into the yard. When he dismounted, he handed his reins to an old cowpuncher who was serving as Jessie's stablehand.

"Any luck finding us a couple of new hands, Ed?" Jessie asked with concern furrowing her brow.

"I'm afraid not," he answered. "Oh, there are cowboys for hire in town, but only men we've either had to let go in the past because they were worthless, or a few drunks, thieves, and general troublemakers."

"I'd rather go into our roundup shorthanded than hire men that will cause us trouble."

"We're about four men short," Ed reminded her. "That's going to make it mighty tough on everyone. I still think that I ought to ride up north to Amarillo and take a look at the cowboys that are hanging around that panhandle country looking for work. There's generally some pretty good hands thereabouts."

"Yes," Jessie conceded, "there are. But that's a long ride and you look a little worn down. I hate to ask you to ride that far just before our roundup."

"No trouble. I can get back a week early and get things organized from here. After a week of that, I'll be ready to ride again."

Ed was in his late fifties, his features weathered and his hands thick from a lifetime of hard ranch work. In the mornings, he suffered from arthritis in all the broken bones he'd received when he was a top young bronc buster. Now, he was one of the finest cattlemen in Texas, and Jessie would not have traded him for anyone. If Ed Wright believed that riding to Amarillo would solve their labor problem, she supposed that he ought to go.

"Could you really return by the end of next week?"

"Why, sure!" Ed promised. "I figure a couple of days to get over there and a couple in Amarillo, and then two

2

more to come back with our new hands. Adds up to six days."

"Give yourself extra time to rest or just be picky with the hiring," Jessie suggested. "I pay top wages, but I expect the best."

"The best aren't easy to find," Ed told her. "They usually start their own little spreads. Those that don't have what it takes will lie and brag and say anything when you're talking to them about the work. They may even talk a good cowboy line, but when it comes to really knowing how to handle themselves on a roundup, there's only one way to find out; and that's to see them in action."

"I know," Jessie said, "but I still say that any man who is good with a rope is likely to be good with cattle and horses. Make them show you their roping skills. That'll be your best single measure of what kind of hands they really are."

"I'll do it, Miz Starbuck," Ed promised. "When do you want me to leave?"

"The sooner the better."

"There's still a lot of daylight left. I could leave within the hour and be in Amarillo tomorrow night, if I push it a little."

"A lot of the big outfits over there will also be looking to add extra cowboys," she warned. "Perhaps it really would be better to go over there right now, even though we won't need them for awhile."

"Well, to my way of thinking, we can weed out any bad ones before the roundup starts, and that'll save us a lot of trouble. If I hire three or four men next week, we'll have a month or so to look them over real good."

"Fine," Jessie said. "I'm going to send Ki with you."

"You know I like him, even though he isn't all that much of a talker."

"You talk enough for two," Jessie said, with a wink that caused her foreman to grin.

"Yeah," Ed admitted, "I expect I do. Where is Ki?"

"I think he's gone for a run."

"I'll never understand that sort of thing. Why would a man run unless he just *had* to?"

"It keeps him in top shape, and you know how important that is to Ki. He's a samurai, Ed. A samurai's code is that of a protector."

"*Your* protector," Ed reminded her. "Not mine."

"He'll protect you because you're my friend," Jessie assured her foreman.

"I guess that's true enough," Ed conceded, "even though I figure I'm plenty old enough to protect myself."

"You may well be, but it's always nice to have a man like Ki riding at your side."

"True enough." Ed remounted his horse. "Well, I'd guess I'd better go out and tell him we'll be leaving in an hour or so. By the way, Miz Starbuck, exactly how many men do you want me to hire?"

"Four, at thirty dollars a month. I figure that we ought to get at least two that are good enough to join the regular crew and help us during the roundup."

"You'd think so, but there are a lot of worthless men that *think* they're cowboys but don't know the difference between a steer and a heifer."

"Be choosy," Jessie advised. "Amarillo ought to have a lot of good men willing to earn top wages."

"I sure hope so," Ed told her as he reined his horse around and put the spurs to its flanks.

4

"So do I," Jessie said to herself, watching him gallop away to find Ki.

Ed only had to ride about a mile before he saw the samurai loping along a ridgeline about three or four miles from the ranch house. "Amazin'," Ed drawled as he spurred his horse.

It took him a half hour to run down the samurai, who wasn't even sweating. When Ki saw the Circle Star foreman, he waved and angled back toward the ranch. Ed kept his horse to a slow trot alongside him.

"Miz Starbuck wants me to ride up to Amarillo and see if I can hire some men for the roundup. She asked for you to come along with me, Ki. Hope you don't mind."

In truth, Ed knew that the samurai *would* mind. Not because he was unwilling to make the long ride north, but because he did not like to leave Jessie without his protection, even when she was at ranch headquarters.

"How long will we be gone?" Ki asked.

"About a week," Ed replied. "Miz Starbuck wants me to leave soon as I can. I can get packed and out of here within the hour. How 'bout you?"

"I'll be ready," Ki said.

"Good. I'll have two fresh horses saddled, the packs filled, and everything in order. All you'll need is yourself and your own belongings. I . . . I suppose you'll also bring those weapons of yours, huh? The backward bow, the arrows, and that other stuff?"

"I will," Ki said, looking offended. "They cause you no harm, and they are important."

Ed patted the gun on his hip. "A sixgun takes a lot less packin', and it sure whittles down the opposition in a big hurry."

5

"Every man should have confidence in his weapons and his ability to use them."

"That's right," Ed replied, not sure whether or not the samurai was being serious or spoofing him. "Anyway, if you need a little extra time, I could . . ."

"One hour is plenty," Ki said before he turned and ran toward the ranch house.

True to his word, Ki was ready to leave in one hour. Jessie came out of the house to wish them a safe and speedy journey and give one last piece of advice.

"Ed, you know that roundup is a tough and demanding time for the crew. There are long hours and not enough sleep. Whoever you hire, make sure that they're up to the mark. If there's any question in your mind, don't hire them. Like I said before, I'd rather be shorthanded than to have some deadbeat hurt somebody else because of his mistakes."

"Right," Ed agreed.

Jessie turned to Ki. "Keep Ed out of trouble."

"He's too old to get into trouble," Ki said with a straight face even while Ed guffawed. "But I'll watch out for him all the same."

"Good. I'll see you and our new cowboys in about a week or ten days."

The Circle Star foreman and the samurai reined their horses north and rode away at a gallop. Jessie watched them for a long time from the elevated station of her front porch. Even though they were only going to be absent for a short time, she knew that she would miss them very much. Ed and Ki were her left and right hands. Without either man, she felt like she'd be greatly handicapped.

When the two riders turned to specks on the northern

6

horizon, Jessie finally turned and went back inside. She must have had a worried look on her face, however, because the maid who helped clean her house broke the silence.

"Do not worry, Miss Starbuck. Those are good men and very strong. They will be safe."

"I'm sure that they will, Abby," Jessie said to the older woman. "But you know how much I depend on them."

"I know," Abby said. "And I know that you wish you could be riding with them right now."

Jessie had to smile at that because it was true. She would have liked nothing better than to ride her favorite palomino, Sun, off to adventure in rough-and-tumble Amarillo. Then she sighed and turned her thoughts back to running the Circle Star.

Chapter 2

The trip north to Amarillo was long but uneventful, and both Ki and Ed were dirty and tired by the time they arrived late in the afternoon. The town was a popular stop for many of the big cattle drives north and it was wide open, often witness to violent gunfights when the cowboys had a little too much to drink in one of the saloons.

"Let's get hotel rooms and hot baths. Then we'll put some good food in our bellies," Ed suggested. "And afterward, I mean to visit some of the saloons and spread the word that I'm looking for experienced cowboys."

"I'll come along with you."

"Thanks, but that won't be necessary. Didn't Miz Starbuck give you a few errands to do while we're here?"

"She did," Ki admitted. "There's Jim Frank, her favorite saddlemaker. I'm supposed to order a saddle and some other things from him. And I guess she also needs a new pair of boots."

8

Ed looked down at the sandals the samurai preferred when not riding. "You ought to have Frank make up a pair for you while we're here. He could have a pair ready in a couple of days."

"I'm fine," Ki told the Circle Star foreman.

"Or go to the gunsmith and see what he'll sell you in the way of a Colt .45 and a Winchester carbine. You'd like owning your own firearms."

Ki knew that the foreman was just teasing him, hoping for some kind of a strong reaction. Ki liked Ed, but he wasn't about to give him the satisfaction. "I'll do just fine with what I have, thank you."

"Sure, you will," Ed said with a wide grin. "And anyone that doesn't think so is in for big trouble."

They left their horses at the best livery in town and hauled their saddlebags and bedrolls up to the Plains Hotel, where they always stayed when in town or delivering cattle to the rail station.

"Nice to see you!" the hotel owner said when they dropped their things at the desk and asked for the registry. "Are we also going to have the pleasure of Miss Starbuck's company tonight?"

"I'm afraid not," Ed replied. "She has a lot of paperwork to do."

"With as many businesses as Miss Starbuck oversees," the hotelman said, "I can imagine she spends a lot of time in her office."

"Not as much as you'd think. Miz Starbuck believes in hiring the best people she can find and giving them top dollar and the authority to make their own decisions."

"Of course she does," the man said. "That's why she has you in charge of her ranch, Ed."

A modest man, Ed blushed with embarrassment.

"Well," he said, "I treat the Circle Star just like it was my own ranch. I try to make the right decisions and make the operation show an annual profit. Miz Starbuck really loves her cattle ranch, and for that I am most grateful."

"And understandably so," the hotelman said. "We've put you in rooms 201 and 202. I'll bill meals and any other expenses to the ranch, same as always. I hope you enjoy your stay in Amarillo."

"We will if we can find some good cowhands," Ed told him. "Anybody around town looking for work?"

"I'm sure there are," the hotelman said reassuringly. "Especially when they find out whom you represent. The word has long been out that Miss Starbuck is willing to pay for the best."

"That's right," Ed agreed. He turned to Ki. "Meet you back down here for dinner in about two hours?"

"Sounds good," the samurai replied.

The owner rang a bell and the bellman appeared.

"Please show Mr. Wright and Ki to their rooms. Make sure that they have fresh baths drawn for them immediately."

"Yes, sir!"

They went upstairs and Ed called to Ki from the doorway to his room, "See you downstairs for dinner in two hours. I'm hungry enough to eat a whole cow by myself. You gonna eat them vegetables like you usually do?"

"I am."

"A little whiskey would ease the pain of your saddle sores," Ed claimed.

"If I had any, I'd use Epsom salt in my bath water."

Ed chuckled. "You are a piece of work, Ki. A real, honest-to-goodness piece of work."

"Thank you," Ki said formally as he went into his room.

Ed turned to the bellman. "I'll tell you one thing: I wouldn't tease him if I was an enemy. He's the kind of man that'll take your head off, hand it to you, and bow before you realize it's even missing."

The bellman's eyes widened and he tried to think of something to say, but words failed him. He just nodded and smiled. Ed tossed him bits and went inside to wait for his bath.

After dinner, Ki went for a walk about town and Ed headed for the row of saloons where he knew he'd find cowboys. Ki didn't drink hard spirits and had never seemed real comfortable in saloons, so Ed was just as glad to be going alone.

Like most cattle towns, Amarillo had its "red light" district, the bad side of the tracks where prostitution and dissipation were not only allowed, they were encouraged. But there was another part of town that catered to a better grade of customer, the townsfolk themselves as well as cowboys with some moral upbringing. In these places, the drinks were considerably more expensive, but they weren't watered down, and the gambling tables were honest.

The barnlike Big Buck Saloon was especially popular with quality men who sought to avoid the drunken rowdiness that prevailed at the lower-class establishments, the steady ranch hands and locals. Ed had been in the place dozens of times and had never seen a hint of drunkenness or trouble. A man could make friends at the Big Buck, but if he preferred his own company, he was left to the solace of his thoughts, no questions asked.

11

"Why, if it isn't Ed Wright!" The bartender, a hale and hearty Irishman named Mike Malone, shouted loud enough to make heads turn all about the room.

"Hello, Mike," Ed answered, as they shook hands. "How you been these days?"

"Business is always good," Mike said, and Ed knew that he wasn't just boasting. "I treat my customers right, they treat me right. It's that simple."

"I wish ranching were that simple," Ed said as Mike drew him a frothy beer. "In fact, that's why I'm here this evening. I'm looking for about four good hands."

"This is the place to find 'em," Mike said. "I run the wild bastards off and only allow those with some manners to drink here. They're the steady ones."

Ed took a long pull on his beer and looked around. "Are all these boys on someone's payroll, or are a few of them looking for work?"

"I couldn't tell you to a man," Mike confessed. "As you know, there are some big ranches up in these parts, and a good cowboy always prides himself on his loyalty. A lot of these boys have been with the same ranch for over ten years."

"Good men leave good jobs for a lot of reasons," Ed argued. "I just need four, Mike. Point me toward 'em."

Mike frowned and surveyed the thirty or more cowboys that were drinking and gambling in the Big Buck. "Well," he said finally, "I don't know those men sitting at that far table, but at least three of them look like seasoned hands."

"They're strangers?"

"Yeah," Mike said. "They've only been coming in here for the last couple of nights. They're real quiet and haven't caused any trouble. Seem polite and well-mannered. You might want to just sound them out about work."

"Thanks," Ed said, "I will." He picked up his beer and sauntered over to the table that Mike had pointed out. Three of the men were obviously cowboys, while the fourth fellow looked like a gambler.

"Howdy," Ed said in greeting. "You boys mind if I have a word with you?"

"Hell, no," one of them replied. "What you got to say?"

Ed introduced himself. "If you're from West Texas, you've no doubt heard of the Circle Star Ranch. You couldn't hardly hire on with a better outfit. But I'm only looking for veteran cowboys."

"How much are you paying?"

"Thirty a month and we feed good. I expect you have your own horses, saddles, and bedrolls."

"We do."

Ed pulled up a chair, realizing he was having a difficult time reading these men. They *looked* like cowboys, but they didn't *feel* like cowboys. Something was not quite right. They were too closemouthed and grim. Sure, they were polite and sober, but too evasive, not offering anything about previous homes, jobs, or bosses.

"Well, what do you boys think? I'd expect to see your stock and I'll have to ask you to show me how you handle a rope. Other than that . . ."

"We'd have to rope to get a job on your damned outfit?" one of the men snapped. "What the hell kind of a test is that?"

Ed blinked, surprised at the sudden heat in the man's

voice. He was big, well over six feet, and the toughest looking of the bunch. Up until this moment, he'd also been the quietest.

"A cowboy has to be good with a rope to work on our roundup," Ed explained.

"Well, what the hell are we supposed to rope in Amarillo? A whore or a dog or something?"

"Quiet, Jim," one of the others said. "There's no need to get all heated up."

But Jim *was* heated up, although Ed could not, for the life of him, imagine why.

"Look," he said, deciding that he and Mike both must have misjudged this bunch, "let's just forget I came over here and offered you boys a job."

"You didn't offer us diddly-shit!" Jim said loudly, coming to his feet and reaching across the table to grab a fistful of Ed's shirtfront. "All you did was sashay over here and tell us we had to show you if we could rope. Like we were dogs that had to sit up for a damned bone!"

"Easy, Jim! Just . . . just ease off the old fella," the gambler warned. "We don't have to do a damn thing. Remember? We're just fine without his job, so let him go."

But Jim cocked his fist. "I'm just sick and tired of sons of bitches like this jerking us around!"

Ed couldn't believe what was happening. He was about to get his head bashed in for no good reason at all.

"Whoa!" a cowboy sitting at a nearby table ordered as he slapped his cards down and unfolded to his feet. "There's no cause for getting all riled up."

"No," Ed agreed. "There sure isn't."

"Butt out!"

But the cowboy didn't butt out. He was also big, though a lot handsomer than the man who'd forced Ed onto the tips of his toes. He looked to be younger, too, maybe only about twenty-one or twenty-two, with sandy hair and dark blue eyes. He was dressed pretty fancy with a leather vest, a new, cream-colored Stetson, and a red silk bandanna. He wore a beautiful tooled leather cartridge belt and holster, both too fancy for a working cowboy and his boots were polished, another indicator that he was not just an ordinary cowpuncher.

"Let go of him," the cowboy said to Jim. "He's old enough to be your father and he deserves some respect."

Jim hunched his bull-like shoulders. "I don't think you were invited to this party. Now just sit back down and you won't get hurt."

Ed caught a glimpse of Mike Malone out of the corner of his eye. He had a shotgun in his fists and a menacing look on his face. When he looked at Jim, there was murder in his expression.

"Let go and step back," Mike ordered, "before I blow your head off."

Jim wasn't fazed by the threat. "If you shoot, you're going to kill us both."

"Jim," one of his buddies said, "this has gone far enough!"

"That's right," the young cowboy agreed. "It has."

What happened next happened very fast. Jim threw Ed aside and took a powerful swing at the fancy cowboy, who ducked, then drove his own fist up like a piston and caught Jim just under the ribs. Jim's face drained of blood and he staggered. The cowboy kicked his feet out from under him and Jim hit the floor with a grunt. Before he could recover, the cowboy put his boot on

15

his throat. Everyone in the room heard his ominous warning.

"I don't know what the hell has gotten into you, and I don't much care. What I do know is that there are saloons that cater to mean sonsabitches like you, and this is not one of them."

"You got that right!" Mike said, before turning to Jim's companions. "Get your friend out of here and don't any of you ever come back!"

They hauled Jim to his feet, and he stabbed a finger at Ed, then at the young cowboy and yelled, "If I see either one of you on the street, you'd better go for your gun, gawdammit, because I'll be goin' for mine."

"Now *that*," the friendly cowboy said, "would be a real fatal mistake."

Ed straightened his shirt and tucked it back into his pants. He looked at the saloon owner. "Thanks, Mike, but next time something like that happens, try not to bring a scatter gun into the fight. It didn't make me breathe any easier, I'll sure tell you."

Mike chuckled. His eyes went from Ed to the young cowboy. "Hey, stranger. My name is Mike Malone and I'm buying you all the drinks that you want tonight."

The cowboy grinned. "I could use a couple."

"So could I," Ed admitted. "Why don't you bring us both a couple of double whiskeys, Mike. In fact, bring us a bottle of your best!"

"Sure enough," Mike called.

Ed led his young friend over to an empty table. "That was quite a punch you laid on that big fella. You ducked and swung and connected all in one motion."

"Thanks," the man said. "By the way, my name is Dustin."

16

"Well, Dustin, you sure weren't afraid of that fella."

"You weren't, either," Dustin said. "Mostly, it seemed you were just shocked that he came on so strong for no good reason."

"That's true."

"I'll bet, in another second or two, you'd have found a way to knee him in the crotch and drop him like a stone."

"I wasn't in a position to do much of anything," Ed admitted. "I could have just shot him in the foot or something, but I didn't want to do that."

"Might have been for the best," Dustin said. "Anyway, I can't figure out either why that big jasper went so crazy."

Mike arrived with glasses and a bottle and Ed poured them drinks. When they were alone again, Ed said, "I can't quite figure you out, Dustin. You sort of look like a cowboy, but then again you look too prosperous. Do you have your own ranch?"

"No," Dustin said, "and I don't even want one."

"Are you even a cowboy?"

"I was."

"Not anymore?"

Dustin shrugged, not answering the question. He had blue eyes and a wide, easy smile. There was a scar running across his brow and his nose had been busted, but not badly. He was the kind of man that Ed took to right away, the kind he was always on the look out for to add to the Circle Star crew.

Ed sipped his whiskey. "Did you hear me telling those others that I was looking for cowboys?"

"I did."

"Are you interested?"

17

"I don't think so. I got bigger fish to fry right now. I hope."

"Too bad," Ed said, "because, if you're a good hand, you could work your way up, and there's no finer spread to work for than Miz Starbuck's."

"*She* owns the ranch that you ramrod?"

"Why, of course. I thought everyone 'round here knew that."

"I'm not from Texas," Dustin said.

"Then that explains it." Ed leaned back in his chair. "So, I'm not one to pry into another man's business, but I will say that I like the way you handle yourself; I think that Miz Starbuck'd like you, too. We might be able to go to thirty-five dollars a month, but you'd have to keep that a secret so's the other men I hire wouldn't get sore."

"Sorry," Dustin said. "Punching cows just isn't what I want to do anymore. Not even for a woman as rich as Miss Jessica Starbuck."

"You've heard of her."

"Yeah, I have." Dustin sipped his drink, barely consuming a drop, only making the gesture so he wouldn't seem ungrateful for Mike's offering. "And I've also heard that she is extraordinarily beautiful."

"She is that," Ed said, his voice guarded. "But she's a real lady."

"Glad to hear it," Dustin said, "because they are becoming fewer and fewer."

"Amen!" Ed grunted in agreement.

They talked for about twenty more minutes, Dustin mostly listening and Ed mostly talking and drinking. Finally, Ed pushed to his feet. He'd maybe had a few more drinks than he'd planned on consuming and he'd definitely spent a lot more time in the Big Buck than he'd planned.

"Well, Dustin, it's time for me to go. I've got to stop by a couple more saloons and spread the word that we're looking for top hands and paying top dollar."

"You shouldn't have a bit of trouble finding all the cowboys you need."

Ed smoothed his shirtfront, the memory of Jim still fresh in his mind. "I hope not, but you never know when you're going to meet up with some crazy like that Jim."

"There are plenty enough of them around, even in the good saloons like this one," Dustin said.

They shook hands and Ed said, "By the way, I never got your last name."

"That's because I never gave it to you."

"Yeah, I guess that's right," Ed admitted. "Anyway, if you change your mind about cowboying, we'll be here another day or two and I'll sign you on."

"After I do a couple of rope tricks?"

Ed stared until he saw that Dustin was trying to hold back a laugh. Then, Ed laughed too. He ended up by saying, "Hell, Dustin, *you* wouldn't have to do any rope tricks. When you threw that punch and saved my hide, you passed the test as far as I'm concerned."

Ed left Dustin then, but he made a mental note to stop by the next night and introduce Ki to the man. Perhaps, between the two of them, they could convince Dustin to change his mind.

The clear night air was a tonic to Ed's reeling senses, and he took several deep breaths before starting down the boardwalk toward the next saloon. He was bone-marrow weary, and decided that he'd only go into a couple of familiar saloons where he was welcome and well known. After that, he'd go back to the hotel and get a long and well-deserved night's rest. He was just passing an alley between two buildings when someone shouted, "Hey!"

Ed just had enough time to turn his head when a powerful hand shot out and grabbed him by the throat. It was Jim! Ed reached for his six-gun, but Jim was already dragging him into the corridor and the darkness.

Ed was old, but he was tough and strong. Trouble was, his eyes hadn't yet adjusted to the darkness, after the bright lights of the Big Buck. Trouble was, too, Jim was about fifty pounds of muscle heavier.

Ed felt a fist slam into the side of his face. His jaw cracked and he tried to stifle a scream as Jim began to beat the hell out of him. Ed kicked and punched for all he was worth, and somehow, with his jaw broken and blood pouring down his face and into his eyes, he managed to break free and throw himself back onto the boardwalk.

"Let him go!" a voice hissed. "You paid him back, now let him go!"

"But I ain't broke his legs yet!"

"Let him go!" the voice insisted.

"Shit!" Jim cursed. "All I broke was his damned jaw! His nose is still in the middle of his face and . . ."

"Come on! You'd have killed that old son of a bitch if I'd let you hit him any more. Now let's go!"

Ed had never heard more welcome words. He'd been whipped a few times in his life, but never worse than now. He took a half-dozen steps and collapsed. His head was spinning and he kept spitting blood, wondering if his ribs were broken and if one of them had punctured his lung.

Somehow, he climbed back to his feet and staggered back into the Big Buck Saloon before he collapsed again.

"Jesus Christ!" Mike Malone bellowed. "Ed!"

Mike and then Dustin were hovering over him, but they were indistinct, their shocked and concerned expressions disjointed and blurry, as if they were looking at him through a fishbowl.

"Who did this?" Dustin was pleading. *"Who did this!"*

Ed tried to speak but couldn't.

"Was it that big man? The crazy one called Jim?"

Ed couldn't speak, but he dipped his chin in assent.

Dustin cursed and then his face vanished. As Ed slipped into unconsciousness, he heard Mike shout, "Kill that crazy bastard!"

And then, faint, as if from a million miles away, Dustin called, "I will!"

★

Chapter 3

Dustin went from one saloon to the next that night, each one a little rougher and seedier than the last. Every time he entered a saloon, he stepped to one side and froze, eyes swiftly canvasing the crowd, looking for the three cowboys and the gambler who had been sitting together at the Big Buck Saloon.

At a sleazy establishment called Fast Mary's, Dustin found his men—or at least all of them except crazy Jim, the one he most wanted. They pretended not to recognize him, which was just fine. He had no bone to pick with them and preferred to leave them alone if they would reciprocate. But first, they had to tell him where Jim was hiding.

"Good evening," Dustin said, thinking that the gambler would be the one to watch closest. He was lean and reptilian, with a proud hooked nose and small, deep-set eyes that missed nothing. He was the first to spot Dustin coming toward the table and give the others a warning.

"Sir, are you addressing this party?" the gambler asked politely.

"Of course I am," Dustin said. "You're the same bunch that were sitting in the Big Buck less than an hour ago with that troublemaker named Jim."

"Are you *sure* that you are not mistaken?"

"I'm damned sure," Dustin growled. "And I'd also like to be sure and say that I got no problems with any of you fellas. I don't know what the hell your game is, but you're up to something shady, I'd bet on that."

The gambler's eyes tightened a little at the corners and his thin lips turned downward in contempt. "Mister," he said, "I think maybe you're drunk. That being the case, I'll excuse your bad manners and allow you to walk out of this saloon intact."

"I'm not drunk," Dustin said. He stepped back, planted his feet a little farther apart and his right hand a little closer to the butt of his gun. "What I *am* is looking for your friend, the big boy that I dropped to the floor after he tried to rough up that older fella. Now, where is he?"

"I don't know what you're talking about," the dangerous one said, an icy grin on his thin lips. "Do you, boys?"

The other two cowboys shook their heads and started to climb to their feet, but Dustin's hand dropped to his six-gun. It came out so fast it caught all three flat-footed.

"Now," Dustin said quietly as the room fell silent and some of the men nearest the front door began to duck outside, "I'm going to ask you one more time to tell me where to find the hole your big, ugly friend crawled inside. And if you *don't* tell me, I'm going to have to get nasty."

23

The gambler slowly came to his feet, hands up and out in front of him so that there would be no misunderstanding his intentions. "Mister," he said, "I don't know who you are, but we've no quarrel with you."

"I'm the man that's going to shoot your balls off," Dustin said, dropping the barrel of his gun until it came in line with the dandy's crotch. "Now, I want to find Jim—right *now*."

"He's in the back room," one of the rough-looking cowboys said. "With a whore."

"What whore and which room?"

"Hell, we don't know!" the man said. "She's just a whore!"

"Her name is Lilly," the gambler said. "Just Lilly."

"Bartender!"

The bartender came up. He was a stout man in his mid-thirties, with a handlebar mustache and only one ear. "If you kill them here," he said, "I'm going to charge you for the trouble it takes to clean up the blood and cart 'em off to the undertaker."

"Which door back there belongs to Lilly?" Dustin asked.

"Second one on the right. But if you happen to kill her by mistake, God hisself won't be able to save your ass from a hanging. Lilly is a favorite."

"I won't make a mistake," Dustin said, turning away and heading for the back door.

He hadn't taken six steps before a gunshot crashed through the room and he swore he felt the hot breath of a bullet zing past his right earlobe. He whirled and saw the gambler drop a snub-nosed derringer and then throw up his hands.

24

"Don't shoot!"

"Why?" Dustin asked. "Because you aimed at my back and missed? You know, you really shouldn't try to use one of those damned pop guns; anything over ten paces, it's all luck, and mister, your's just went sour."

The gambler began to sweat. Big globs materialized on his face and he swallowed loudly.

"I'm not armed," he said. "You'd be shooting down a defenseless man."

"Defenseless as a rattlesnake." Dustin walked up to the frightened gambler. "You're a con man and two-bit gambler if I ever saw one. Take off your fancy jacket and roll up your sleeves!"

"What?"

"You heard me!"

The man did as he was told while Dustin lined the other pair up where he could keep a good eye on them. "And I'll bet you boys are the decoys and the spotters. Huh? Bet neither one of you ever cowboyed in your life. You just dress up and play the part and drag in the saloon suckers for your friend to fleece like sheep. Isn't that right?"

"Who the hell are you, mister?" one of the cowboy-types wanted to know. "The new town marshal or somethin'?"

Dustin shook his head. "No, I'm not the law. But if I were, I'd run you out of Amarillo faster than your friend here can deal from the bottom of a marked deck."

By now, the dandy had his coat off but he was extremely reluctant to roll up his sleeves. "Why don't you just let this pass?"

"Not until you show the folks in this fine establishment

the kind of game you were planning to play. Now, roll up those sleeves!"

The gambler finally did as told. He was wearing garters on his forearms, and they held not only aces and kings, but also a device that would snap the card down along the wrist and into the cheat's cupped hand.

"Well, boys," Dustin said to everyone in the saloon, "I wanted you to see what kind of a man you'd be playing against. Maybe some of you will take it upon yourselves to escort these three 'gentlemen' out of town."

"On a rail!" a drunken cowboy yelled.

"If we ever cross paths again, I'll kill you!" the gambler shouted. "You'll be a dead man!"

Dustin paid the man no mind as he and his two "cowboy" friends were overwhelmed and "escorted" out of the saloon. Dustin started back toward the crib where he knew he'd find Jim with the whore named Lilly.

"If you just bust in there," a regular warned, "and if that big fella don't kill you, Lilly might. She's a whole lot more accurate with a pistol than that cardsharp that you got the drop on just a minute ago."

"Is that a fact?"

"One that's gotten more than one son of a bitch plugged," the man said with a knowing look.

Dustin took his advice and kept his six-gun firmly in hand as he pushed through Lilly's door. Big Jim was ready, willing, and able to take his pleasure and Lilly was just about to accommodate him when Dustin burst in.

"What the hell!" Lilly cried. "Mister, you gotta stand outside and wait your damned turn!"

"Hello, Jim," Dustin said, gun in hand, kicking the

26

door shut. "I guess I caught you at a real bad moment here, huh?"

"What do you want?" Jim snarled, rearing up on his haunches.

"You just beat the living hell outta of that old cowboy. You dragged him into the alley and really gave him the once over, didn't you?"

"Mister, I don't know what the hell you're talkin' about!"

"Stand up."

Jim hopped off the bed.

"Turn and face the wall," Dustin ordered.

"Huh?"

"Turn, dammit!"

Jim turned so that he was faced sideways. "Say adios to your dick," Dustin told the man in a pleasant voice.

"What . . ."

Dustin's gun bucked in his fist, and although it was loud, it didn't begin to match the scream that filled the room as Jim grabbed at what had been a huge erection.

"Jeezus! You shot the son of a bitch clean off!" Lilly screeched, looking horrified. "You castrated him!"

Jim stared at the blood pouring from his mangled manhood, then fainted dead away.

"I took pity on him," Dustin said. "I should have killed the bastard by all rights. That's what he almost did to a man old enough to be his father who gave him no cause for trouble. Maybe now he'll calm down and become more reasonable. Works with horses. A gelding is always a lot easier to get along with than a stud." He holstered his gun as if nothing unusual had happened.

Lilly glanced at Jim, then back to Dustin. "If he bleeds to death, you'll swing for murder."

"He won't 'bleed to death,' Lilly. Not if you wrap a towel around what's left of his dick."

"Ain't enough to wrap a damn handkerchief around!"

Dustin turned to leave, saying over his shoulder, "You tell Jim that if he and his friends aren't out of Amarillo by sunrise, I'll hunt them down and kill 'em."

"Who are you?" Lilly cried. *"What* are you?"

"I'm a Texas tornado," Dustin replied. "You never know what I might do next. And I'm your best friend or your worst enemy, depending." He stopped at the door and turned to face her. "Lilly?"

"Yeah?"

"You're getting too damned old for this line of work."

"I'm only twenty-six," she replied sullenly, dragging the sheet off the bed. Jim moaned as she tried to apply the makeshift bandage, but didn't regain consciousness.

"You look ten years older. Find a good man and settle down before you get the pox or some drunk cuts you up or kills you for a few dollars."

Lilly's face transformed into a slow smile. "So that's how it's done? Just like that?"

"That's how it's done."

"How come you know so damned much? You're no older than I am."

"I've packed a lot of living into a short but exciting lifetime," Dustin explained. "And I hate bullies and cardsharps and anybody else who takes advantage of weaker people."

"I don't believe any of this is happening," Lilly said. "This is all like a dream. One minute this big, ugly cowboy is about to use me, the next minute you're shooting his equipment off. What's it all coming to?"

28

Dustin chuckled. "Where can I find the best doctor in town, Lilly?"

"That'd be Dr. Branch. Feeling guilty for what you done to this ornery bastard?"

"Nope; the doc needs to attend to that old cowboy Jim beat the living hell out of."

"Dr. Branch lives just up the street. You can't miss his office sign. But he'll be damned mad about being woke up at this hour."

"Damned mad means he'll probably charge me about double what he would if he was in a good mood. Right?"

"Right."

"Well, Lilly, since this fella never had a chance to do what he came for, I guess you ought to give me his money so I can pay the doctor."

"Not a chance."

Dustin studied Lilly. She was short, with dark hair and large breasts. Her hips were wide, her thighs heavy, but she was still quite handsome—and quite unconcerned about her nakedness.

"If you won't give me the money," Dustin said, "then I'll just have to come back and collect what poor Jim there won't ever again be man enough to."

"You serious?"

"I am."

Lilly expelled a deep breath. "Well, then you just do that," she said after several moments of consideration. "But if you get trigger-happy with me, I'll make sure that you end up in even worse shape than Jim."

"I'd never mistreat a woman, not even a whore," Dustin assured her.

"You're a real prince," Lilly said with a heavy layer of sarcasm in her voice. "Now go get the doctor. After

29

he's had a chance to look at your friend, send 'im over here."

"Whatever you say, Lilly."

She studied him for a moment, and then she burst into nervous laughter. "Mister, you really *are* a Texas tornado!"

"Told you," Dustin said as he disappeared out the door.

★

Chapter 4

Dustin found Dr. Branch's office in less than two minutes. It was locked and the windows were shuttered, so he began to pound on the door loud enough to shake the entire building.

"Go away!" a groggy voice pleaded.

"Doc, there's a man that's been hurt real bad. We need your help."

"Come back in the morning."

Dustin reared back and kicked in the door. It slammed open, and Dustin shouted, "Doc, get out here or I'm going to find you and drag you out of bed!"

The doctor appeared as if by magic. He was thin to the point of being cadaverous and looked dissipated. He smelled of whiskey and tobacco.

"If you're the best doctor in Amarillo," Dustin growled, "I'd sure hate to meet your competition."

"Shut up," Branch hissed. "What the hell can't wait until morning?"

Dustin told him about Ed Wright. "He's pretty badly

31

beaten up, Doc. He's not a young man and needs your help."

"You payin' for my services?"

"No," Dustin said, "but my friend's the foreman of the Circle Star Ranch. I guess you've heard about that outfit and about its owner, Miss Jessica Starbuck. They've got a reputation for paying well. Don't worry, Doc; if you fix up her foreman, you'll be handsomely rewarded."

"Humph," the doctor said, scratching under his nightshirt. "Okay, I'll be right along."

"There's one other little thing you'll need to attend to," Dustin said, a bit reluctantly. "There's a man that's been shot over at Fast Mary's. His name is Jim."

"Sounds like I better take a look at him first and then look at your friend. Nobody ever died of a broken jaw. Where'd this Jim fella get shot?"

"Well," Dustin said, "nobody's gonna pay you to patch him up, so I'd appreciate it if you'd just pull on a pair of pants, grab your shoes and your medical kit and come along with me to look at that foreman."

"I still want to know about the fella that got shot. Where . . ."

"Doc," Dustin said, grabbing the man and spinning him around and then gently shoving him back toward his bedroom. "Just get dressed and I'll explain everything after you've seen Ed."

The doctor was fully awake now. He looked at Dustin and then shrugged. "All right, young man. It appears that I don't have much choice in this matter."

"You'll be well paid, Doc."

Dr. Branch straightened and looked down at Ed Wright. "Well, I can't tell you anything that you probably haven't already figured out for yourself, Mr. Wright. You have a broken jaw. You must have taken one hell of a punch. Fortunately, I think it's a clean break. I've tried to set it right again, but it's going to take some time to heal. That means you'll have to go on pretty much a liquid diet—soups and puddings and porridges for about three months."

Ed groaned.

"You got two cracked ribs and some bad bruises. I stitched up that cut on your temple; shouldn't give you any more trouble. If you weren't in pretty good shape, you might have died from the pounding."

Ed's eyes were swollen almost completely shut. He motioned for Dustin to come nearer and then reached into his pocket and pulled out a pad of paper.

"You need a pencil or pen?"

Ed nodded that he did.

Dustin found a pencil, and Ed scribbled: TELL THE DOCTOR CIRCLE STAR WILL PAY HIM WELL.

"I already told him that."

WHAT ABOUT THAT BIG BASTARD WHO DID THIS TO ME?

"The doctor is going to see him next, but the Circle Star won't pay for that. I guess I'll have to."

WHAT DID YOU DO TO HIM?

Dustin grinned. "I shot off his dick."

Dr. Branch, busy packing his medical kit, was so startled by Dustin's words that he spilled a package of bandages across the floor. He spun around, grabbed the bedpost for support, and said, "You shot off his dick!"

"Not all of it. He'll still be able to piss. I met a man once who had his dick cut off by a whore. He said he could do everything but screw. Damned inconvenient,

33

but he said he managed to still enjoy the women."

Branch collected his spilled bandages. "I need a stiff drink before I go see the man."

"Suit yourself," Dustin said, turning back to Ed. "Anything else I can do for you?"

Ed begin to scribble. I NEED TO HIRE YOU AND THREE TOP-NOTCH COWBOYS.

"I'd cost too much money."

NAME YOUR PRICE.

"A hundred dollars a month."

IF MISS STARBUCK WON'T PAY, I WILL.

"That'd be mighty generous of you," Dustin said, patting Ed on the shoulder. "But I wouldn't allow you to bankrupt yourself. I will come to the Circle Star, though, just to see the place and the famous lady. Ed, is there anything else I can help you with tonight?"

WAKE UP KI AT THE PLAINS HOTEL. ROOM 202. TELL HIM TO COME HERE.

"Who is Ki?"

MY COMPANION AND MISS STARBUCK'S AIDE.

"All right," Dustin said. "Room 202. I'll do it."

"What about that fella at Fast Mary's?" the doctor said when they were outside under the stars again.

"Oh, yeah," Dustin said. "Well, come along and we'll see if he's awake yet."

"Is he likely to be violent?"

Dustin thought about that. "Violent? Well, I expect he's not going to be in a real good mood once he sees that he's been fundamentally altered. But I doubt he's going to be violent. You might want to just tell the ornery son of a bitch that it'll grow back bigger than ever."

"That's ridiculous!"

34

"He probably won't know better, so he'll want to believe," Dustin reasoned. "I'm just trying to think of a way to break the news a little easier."

The doctor looked like he was on his way to the gallows as they traipsed across town and finally went into Fast Mary's. Jim was awake and the bleeding had stopped, but he was in considerable pain and getting drunk just as fast as he could choke the whiskey down. When he saw Dustin, he went crazy and tried to sit up, but the pain was too intense.

"I'll kill you!" he screamed over and over. "I'll kill you!"

"You can try, but it'd be a mistake," Dustin said calmly.

"Doc, sew it back on!"

Dr. Branch looked at the wound and turned around. His hand snaked into his coat pocket for a flask of whiskey, and he gave himself a very liberal dose. Squaring his shoulders, he turned back to face Jim.

"I'm afraid that there is nothing much left to sew back on," he said. "I'll stitch it up best I can. Maybe it just might . . . it might grow back bigger than ever."

Jim's face went from horrid to happy. "Really?"

"There's always a chance," the doctor hedged.

"Bigger than ever?"

The doctor looked away and took another hefty drink of whiskey. "The human body is a wondrous thing the way it recovers and compensates."

"Thank gawd!" Jim cried, before he began to weep. The doc went to his bag for a needle and thread, and Dustin strolled back down the hall looking for Lilly. A harried-looking saloon girl directed him to another room. He rapped loudly on the door.

35

"Who is it?"

"The Texas Tornado."

The door opened at once. Lilly had cleaned up and sprinkled herself with sweet-smelling toilet water. Her hair was combed and brushed and she had applied lipstick. She was wearing a black negligee, which flattered her immensely.

"I was hoping you'd come back and get what Jim paid for," she said as he entered the room.

Dustin locked the door and unbuckled his gunbelt. He re-buckled it and slung it over the bedpost. Then he lifted his arms and Lilly rushed into them, hugging his neck and kissing his mouth.

"You're pretty frisky for a whore," Dustin said with a grin. "Most of 'em just spread 'em wide and lay like corpses."

"You're different," she said, unbuttoning his shirt and pulling it off; her fingers began to work at the buttons of his fly. "You're *real, real* different."

Dustin laughed. When she extracted his manhood, he gently pushed her down between his knees and let her work him up to a froth with her tongue and mouth.

Lilly was good, and even more remarkable, she was excited. Dustin could see the passion in her eyes and hear her rapid breathing as he pulled her up, eased her onto the bed, and mounted her with no preliminaries.

"Oh, yes," she panted, "do me like a Texas tornado! Spin me up and up and then scatter me to the winds!"

Dustin laughed and then he got serious with the lovemaking. It took awhile because Lilly was not used to acting like a normal woman. But after a while, he had her begging for it in earnest and bucking under him like a filly being rode for the first time.

36

When Dustin came, Lilly moaned with pleasure and her own body twitched as she reached her threshold of pleasure. Afterward, he got up and dressed.

"Stay the night," she begged. "You got no place better to go than in me."

"I'd like to do that, Lilly. I really would. Maybe I'll come back before daylight, or tomorrow night."

"I might be busy with someone else," she said, unable to hide her disappointment. "I'm a working woman, you know."

"I know. Only with me, you don't have to work or pretend or anything, do you, Lilly?"

"No," she admitted, coming off the bed and hugging him tightly. "Will you be staying in Amarillo for awhile?"

"I can't."

"But why?"

"I'm a restless man, and I've made some enemies here. They're the kind that'd like nothing better than to ambush me from a rooftop or an alley. I need to move along."

"But you'll come back, won't you?" Lilly asked, not caring that she sounded desperate, even shameless.

"I'd come back to see you," he said. "But I'd hope that you'd found a good husband by then. If you did, I'd pretend I was a cousin or something so he wouldn't get jealous or anything. I'd want you to have a good life, raise a family."

"I'd never forget you," Lilly confessed. "You're . . . you're just real different."

"I guess I am," he admitted, and then he kissed her on the mouth and went to find the sleeping samurai.

Chapter 5

Someone banged loudly against the door of room 202. Ki was instantly awake. He came out of bed and grabbed his *tanto* knife, slipping it out of its sheath.

"Who is it?"

"Name is Dustin," the voice said. "Ed Wright has been hurt real bad. He asked me to come get you."

"Who are you?"

"Right now, I'm just a fella that needs some sleep. Open the damned door."

Ki unlocked the door and stepped aside quickly in case this was some kind ruse to do him physical harm. He'd made more than a few enemies protecting Jessica Starbuck's life and property over the past years, and he had grown especially wary of strangers that came in the night.

Dustin squinted into the darkness of the room and saw a tall, slender oriental-looking man dressed in a pair of black silk pajamas. "You're Ki?"

"I am."

"Name's Dustin. Ed told me you're his companion and Miss Starbuck's aide. You're not what I expected."

"Where is Ed and what's wrong with him?"

Dustin explained the situation in as few words as possible.

Ki's expression was grim. "Later, I want you to tell me the name of the man that did this to him."

"Well," Dustin said, "I'll be happy to do that. But if you're thinking about getting even, I already beat you to it. I shot off his dick and generally taught him some manners."

Ki had been going out the door, but now he stopped, turned, and said, "You what?"

Dustin repeated himself, then added, "This Jim fella isn't going to be causing anyone else problems for quite a while. But you're sure welcome to have what's left of him for target practice. But then, I can see that you aren't even carrying a pistol."

Ki had neither the time nor the inclination to explain. He was furious, more with himself than with Ed's attacker because protecting the Circle Star Ranch foremen had been his responsibility. Now, with Ed incapacitated just a few weeks before the all-important spring roundup, Ki knew that it would put a tremendous extra burden on Jessica. And it was all his fault for not accompanying Ed to the various saloons tonight.

"Hey, wait up," Dustin called, hurrying down the hallway. "I'll stop by and see Ed again. I told him I'd hire on, but not permanent or anything. And I promised I'd find you some real good cowboys, since you're shorthanded."

"We'll take care of that," Ki said over his shoulder.

"Well, now," Dustin replied, "I gave your friend my word I'd help."

"You've done enough already."

"I should have guessed that Jim fella would ambush Ed," Dustin said. "Actually, I thought he'd jump me instead. I feel bad about Ed's busted jaw and ribs. Doc said that Jim might have killed a lesser man with that beating."

Ki was almost running when he hit the street, but then he realized that he didn't even know the doctor's name, much less where his office was or where to find Ed.

"This way," Dustin said, leading them up the dark street. "Doc Branch fixed Ed up, but he's probably still patchin' up Jim. He looks real seedy and probably drinks too damn much, but most of the good ones do. Hell, the bad ones do, too, for that matter. But Doc Branch took good care of Ed, and he's been promised top dollar. I expect you ought to tell Miss Starbuck it was worth twenty or thirty bucks for his services."

"Just shut up," Ki snapped.

"Well, damn!" Dustin exclaimed. "What's the matter with you? I was just trying to lay things out clear. Ed can't even talk. He just writes on a pad. Doc says that the remarkable thing is that Ed didn't get a concussion."

When they reached Ed's side, he was asleep. Dr. Branch was there, tipping up his flask and emptying it. "I gave your friend some opium for the pain," he explained. "He'll be out until well into tomorrow."

"Can he travel?" Ki asked.

"I suppose, but not for a couple of days, at least. Those ribs and that broken jaw would certainly give him fits on the back of a horse."

"I'll buy a wagon with good springs," Ki said, "put

40

a mattress in it, and make it just as comfortable as possible."

"Is it really that important that he get back?" the doctor asked.

"Yes, it is."

"Very well. If his condition improves the way I hope, you can leave Amarillo in two days. But I make no promises."

"Why did that man go after him like that?" Ki asked.

"I don't know," Dustin said. "I think he was one of those fellas that get vicious when drunk. Hell, I didn't even think he was drunk until later. But I've also seen men like that who can be drunk as loons and look stone cold sober."

"Then it wasn't someone that had a grudge against Ed?"

"Nope," Dustin said. "This big Jim fella got all upset when Ed said that he wanted to see how a man roped before he'd hire him. Jim was just spoiling for a fight. He's the kind that likes to hurt people."

"And you shot his manhood away?"

"I did," Dustin confessed. "And I think it will cause him to reflect on his mean and intemperate nature and seek to improve himself."

Upon hearing this, the doctor almost choked.

"Did I say something funny?"

"No, sir!" Doc Branch swore. "Not a thing."

Dustin stretched and yawned. "It's been a long night. Be light in a few hours. I reckon I'm going to bed and get some sleep. Good night."

At the door, Dustin turned back to both men, but it was the samurai whom he addressed. "Ki, I don't quite understand your role here, but it's clear enough that you aren't a cowboy; so I'm going to do the hiring for Miss Starbuck because that's what Ed asked me to do."

"The Circle Star only wants top hands." A pause. "Are you a 'top hand?' "

"I can pull my own freight," Dustin assured him. "I've cowboyed when I couldn't find easier work to do and times were lean."

"Can you rope?"

"I can. And I can ride, fight, and shoot. I can brand cattle, doctor 'em, too. I can fork a bronc and eat camp food and get by on damn little sleep. I can be as tough as the next man—even a shade tougher."

Ki studied him with unconcealed suspicion. "You helped Ed and I know that Miss Starbuck will be grateful. But what we need are cowboys, not gunfighters or troublemakers."

"I don't *make* fights," Dustin said, feeling his hackles rise. "I finish them. You'd do well to keep that in mind, Ki."

After Dustin left, the doctor said, "How am I going to get paid?"

"I'll pay you cash before we leave," Ki assured the man.

"I'm going to have to be with your friend twenty-four hours a day between now and then. I'm afraid I'm going to have to charge you accordingly."

Ki understood. It was a fact that when people found out that they had tapped into the Starbuck wealth, they charged double or triple their usual rate. Ordinarily, Ki would have protested and worked out something reasonable, but not in this case. He would pay the overage out of his own pocket because he felt responsible for what had happened to poor Ed.

"You should have thanked that young fella," the doctor was saying. "Just a few more blows to the face and I think this old fella would have been finished."

Ki nodded and found a chair. "I'll be staying here," he said. "With you and Ed."

The doctor was not pleased. "That's not going to be necessary. Go back to your room and get some rest. I'm sure you've got other business in Amarillo that needs taking care of."

"I'm staying," Ki repeated, studying his good friend's almost unrecognizable features.

The doctor opened his mouth to protest, but changed his mind and clamped his jaw shut. "You suit yourself. Dustin won't have any trouble finding top hands willing to work on a ranch with a reputation like the Circle Star. I expect that he'll probably have men crowding around him when the word gets out about the pay. Thirty dollars a month is about ten dollars above the going rate for top cowboys."

But Ki wasn't listening. He was thinking about Ed and about this new man Dustin, whom he felt uneasy about despite the role the stranger had played in saving Ed Wright's life.

I should have been the one to help Ed, not a stranger, Ki thought. *And that's why I don't like this cocky stranger who seems to have no name, no past.* "Do you know anything about that man?" he asked.

"You mean Dustin?"

"Yes. Do you even know his last name?"

"Never met him before in my life. But I tell you one thing, I've been listening to the talk. About how he helped your foreman at the Big Buck Saloon, and about what happened at Fast Mary's. They say Dustin

43

has no fear. That he acted as if he had ice water in his veins."

"Is that right?"

"That's right. He drew his gun so fast at the Big Buck Saloon he got the drop on this slick gambler and his friends. Caught them standing there flat-footed and made 'em eat crow. Then he exposed the cheatin' device the gambler had up his sleeve and all hell broke loose."

"Dustin seems to have made quite an impression on you and the rest of Amarillo."

"Oh, he has! In one night, he's earned himself a reputation that won't soon be forgotten. If we were holding elections tomorrow for our town marshal, he'd win hands down."

"Even though you don't know his last name, much less his background?"

"To hell with names and background! He stood up against four tough men at the Big Buck Saloon and then saved your friend out in the street. I figure that actions are more important than a man's name or his past. Wouldn't you say so?"

"Yes," Ki said quietly. "I certainly would."

★

Chapter 6

Dustin was not sure why he had bitten into this Circle Star Ranch business except that he had been hearing about the Starbuck family for years; this was going to be his one big opportunity to meet what many called the richest and most beautiful woman in the West. He had read about the Starbuck empire and knew that it was global. Dustin even recalled that Jessie's father was named Alexander and he had started his amazing career in a tiny import business located on the notorious San Francisco waterfront.

Now Jessica Starbuck had full control of the great man's empire, but she preferred the life of a Texas cattle rancher to that of traveling the world in search of new industries and opportunities to exploit and turn into an even greater fortune.

So Dustin would not have missed the opportunity to meet the famous woman and to accept her gratitude for saving the life of her old foreman. And so what if the samurai was suspicious of his background and his motives? Perhaps Ki was Miss Starbuck's jealous lover. In fact, the more that Dustin thought about it, that was probably the real reason for the man's coolness.

Dustin went to the printer's office and had fifty fliers made up to announce that, tomorrow morning at eight o'clock sharp, he would be interviewing cowboys for the Circle Star Ranch. They had to be top hands and know how to work a big roundup.

"Better put the wages on this thing," the printer said. "There's more work than men in this panhandle country right now. We lost a lot of boys in the war."

"Top wages for top men," Dustin promised. "I'm betting that the name 'Circle Star' will be enough of an attraction."

"Might be at that," the printer said. "This will cost you three dollars even."

Dustin paid the bill out of his own pocket, although he was getting pretty short of ready cash. Never mind that. He had a feeling that he was going to be in the chips before too much longer.

Dustin spent that night with Lilly and didn't get nearly enough rest. So he overslept, and by the time he was dressed and out on the street, there were at least a dozen impatient cowboys waiting to talk to him about working for the Circle Star.

"Dammit, it's almost ten o'clock," one tall, tough-looking cowboy groused. "That flier you sent out said to be here by eight! Where the hell were you, anyway?"

"Screwing Lilly," Dustin said. "Sorry."

The tall cowboy's attitude took a big turn. "Shucks," he drawled, "I been with Lilly a time or two. She always kicked me out of her bed after about an hour. So if she

46

let you stay all night and mornin', then I reckon that I'm a lot more jealous than mad."

"What's your name?"

"Lester Morris."

"Are you good?"

"Few better. I was taught to rope by an old vaquero named Gabriel Escobar. I can rope a damn sparrow on the fly."

"What about cattle?"

"I love the sonsabitches," Lester said. "I love to slap a branding iron to their hides, kick the shit outta 'em when they misbehave, and eat 'em when I sit down to the table."

"Then you're hired," Dustin said. "A man has to know how to rope and he has to like beef, dead or alive."

And so the interviews went. Only when Dustin had finished did one of the men that he didn't hire get angry. "Mister," the man growled, "I've worked the best ranches in Oklahoma, Colorado, and Arizona. But I can't seem to hook on with a good ranch down here in Texas to save my ass."

"Then leave the state," Dustin advised. "Go back to where you came from."

"You Texans are such a bunch of dumb sonsabitches that I just might have to do that."

Dustin had been turning away but now he stopped and slowly pivoted on his heels. "Did you say that *we* were dumb?"

"As a post." The man was big and his nose was fist-busted. He looked tough and was spoiling for a fight.

"Down in Texas," Dustin said, "we don't take kindly to people comin' in from the outside and calling us dumb sonsabitches. No, sir, we don't take well to that at all."

"Tough shit."

Dustin saw that the other cowboys were watching. Those that he hadn't hired didn't matter, but the three that he had counted plenty. The last thing Dustin wanted was to ride back to the Circle Star and have those three tell everyone else on the ranch that the Texas Tornado was really nothing more than a puff of hot air.

Dustin reached into his pocket and found a coin. It was a dollar, but it might just as well have been a dime or a gold eagle.

"See this?" he asked the big, belligerent cowboy.

"Sure."

"Watch."

Dustin dropped the coin to the ground between them. The cowboy looked down with a question mark in his eyes and that's when Dustin's right hand whipped up from about knee-level and caught him alongside the jaw. The big cowboy grunted. His eyes crossed as Dustin's left hand chopped down and caught him just behind the ear. The man dropped as if he'd been poleaxed. His face struck the hard street and the breath blasted from his lungs.

Dustin reached down and picked up the dollar. He wiped the dust off of it on his pants and looked at the other cowboys. Flipping the coin into the air, he caught it and dropped it into his pocket.

"That works every time you come across some dumb bastard that can't take his eyes off a little money. You ought to try it for yourself."

The cowboys, those hired and those not, all chuckled in agreement. Dustin glanced at the three he'd hired and said, "We'll probably be leaving tomorrow morning. If I was you boys, I'd get my things in order. You might not get back this way for a good long while."

"Might not ever *want* to get back this way," Lester said, stepping over the unconscious cowboy. "Where'd you learn to throw a punch behind the ear like that?"

"My daddy taught me when I was just a shaver," Dustin said. "He taught me about the coin thing, too. It's like if you dropped a kernel of corn between a chicken's feet. They just naturally can't resist looking. It will give you time for one clean shot. But if you take your best one and it doesn't put your man down, you're in trouble."

Lester chuckled. "I'll remember that. I sure the deuce will!"

Dustin headed back to Lilly's room. He'd promised to take her to breakfast and then they'd spend the day together in rapturous and sweaty union. It seemed the only intelligent way to spend his last day in Amarillo, since the best he'd get at the Starbuck outfit was the company bunkhouse.

Chapter 7

True to his word, Ki found a very good wagon with an excellent pair of springs. He bought a mattress from their hotel and laid it out in the wagon bed.

"I think we're all ready," Ki said.

Doc Branch was not pleased. "I really believe you ought to wait for a few more days," he said, examining Ed for about the tenth time that morning. "You can't promise that this wagon won't have to run over a bunch of potholes."

TO HELL WITH POTHOLES! Ed scribbled. I WANT TO GET BACK TO THE RANCH!

Doc Branch glanced at the scribbled message that Ed thrust before him and then grunted, "I don't much care what you want, you old badger. And even though you might be able to bear the jarring that I know you're going to take even with that mattress, I'm telling you that those ribs won't mend unless they are absolutely immobilized."

GOOD-BYE DOC!

"Damn!" Branch swore, giving up. "You're a stubborn old cuss. But this is going to cost you an extra week or two in bed, or those ribs might just never mend properly. Is that what you want?"

HOW MUCH DO WE OWE YOU, DOC?

"Fifty dollars, mostly for aggravation," Branch snapped. He motioned to the cowboys. "All right, get him out of my sight and into that wagon."

The three new hires, along with Dustin and Ki, all grabbed ahold of the makeshift litter that the doctor had given them to move Ed. In less than three minutes, the foreman was resting comfortably in the back of the wagon. The new men gathered up their horses and swung into their saddles. The supplies and Jessie's new pair of boots were packed around Ed to steady him for the trip back down to the Circle Star.

Ki jumped up onto the driver's seat and took the lines. He looked back over his shoulder at the foreman. "You ready?"

Ed nodded. He looked pale and his cheeks were hollow. The new diet that was being forced upon him was going to take him down to nothing, Ki thought. But Ed was tough. He'd gain back the weight, and he'd be ready for the fall branding.

"Let's go," Ki called, as he snapped the lines down. He knew that it would take a whole day longer to get back to the ranch because of the wagon. His and Ed's horses were tied to the back, and their pace would necessarily be slow, made even more so because of the care it would take to try and avoid jarring Ed unnecessarily.

Some of the townspeople and more than a few cowboys waved good-bye to them as they started through Amarillo. They were near the end of main street and far beyond the train station when a shot rang out. Several men shouted, and when the samurai raised his head, he saw Dustin spurring back up the street.

"What happened?" Lester shouted.

"Someone winged Dustin!"

"Who?"

"Damned if I know, but he better be lookin' for a place to hide."

Dustin had caught the glint of metal shining from the loft of a large barn that housed buggies and wagons. Someone had been there waiting to ambush, and Dustin suspected that it would either be Jim or that gambler he'd exposed as a cheat. And maybe it was the both of them. No matter, they would be scrambling down from the loft and fleeing like rats in a flood.

A silhouette appeared in the doorway of the barn, and it was big enough to tell Dustin that the would-be assassin was Jim. Jim stood his ground, hunched over with pain, and began to fire with his six-gun. Dustin leaned as flat as he could against his horse Charlie's neck and spurred it right at the man. A bullet creased Charlie's shoulder and his stride broke, but he kept running. Dustin saw big Jim throw down his empty gun and begin to run.

"Yaahhh!" Dustin shouted into his horse's ear.

Dustin had owned the big black animal for almost two years. Charlie wasn't the fastest horse in the world, and he could be cantankerous and ill-tempered, but there was no question about either his stamina or his heart. And now, with his shoulder flowing with fresh blood, Charlie seemed to realize that the big man in the doorway of the barn was an enemy. Ears back, teeth bared, Charlie didn't even slow down as he hit Jim and ran right over him.

Jim screamed and rolled. Somehow, he came to his feet, both hands clutching his crotch. "I give!" he cried. "No more!"

Dustin dragged his horse to a sliding stop and jumped off. He drew his gun and said, "Who else was with you in this? The crooked gambler?"

"No!"

"You're a liar!" Dustin shot Jim in the shoulder. The big man howled as the impact of the bullet knocked him backwards.

"Who else!"

"Nobody!" Jim's face was gray. He clutched his ruined privates with one hand and tried to staunch the flow of blood from his shoulder with the other hand. "Look at what you done to me, dammit!"

"It's not my fault that you're a rotten son of a bitch and an even worse shot!"

Dustin intended to say more but he saw a trickle of dust and straw seeping through the board floor of the loft above. "Your friend is still up there, isn't he?"

"No."

Dustin drew back the hammer of his gun. "You better not lie to me again."

"All right! He's up there!" Jim screeched. "And I hope he shoots your guts out!"

Dustin didn't need to take aim, only to pull the trigger. His Colt bucked in his fist, and Jim took a bullet in the heart and slammed over backward. Dustin turned his full attention on the ladder that led up to the loft.

"Gambler!" he shouted. "Gambler, I know you're up

there! Throw down your gun and come on down with your hands up."

"Come and get me!"

"I'll do that," Dustin said, removing his bandanna and pressing it to his own wound, a deep furrow in the flesh just above his right elbow. His shirt was ruined and he was bleeding like a stuck hog, but the wound wasn't fatal. Mostly, it was going to make him stiff and sore for a few weeks. For sure it would take most of the pleasure out of roping and working at the Circle Star roundup.

Ki suddenly appeared. He took one look at the dead man and said, "What happened?"

"That's the fella that beat your foreman up so bad. I guess he just didn't want to go through life a damned eunuch. Maybe I wouldn't have, either."

"Let me see that wound of yours."

"Later," Dustin said. "There's another snake in the hayloft to settle with."

Ki looked upward. "Where?"

Dustin pointed. "That's where I saw a little straw come tricklin' through, but he's probably moved since then."

"I'll take him," Ki said. "You've already done enough. Go find the doctor before you bleed to death."

"The hell with that!" Dustin strode over to the ladder, but when he raised his arms to climb, he winced with pain. "Maybe," he said, looking over at Ki, "you'd like to go up and take care of this fella. Here, you can use my gun. It's got a hair trigger."

"I don't need it."

"You got a hideout gun, or what?"

But Ki wasn't listening. He knew that the man up in the loft would be completely focused on the ladder and that whoever went up it would have the top of their skull blown off before they could make any attempt to strike back. Therefore, it seemed obvious that he had to get up there by some other path.

Ki hurried outside and saw a rope attached to a short boom and pulley, obviously used to raise bales of hay or heavy sacks of grain off a wagon and swing them into the loft for handling and stacking.

Lester had galloped over, and Ki motioned for the cowboy to be silent and to dismount. To his credit, Lester didn't say a word. He climbed down from his horse and held the animal while the samurai jumped up into the saddle and then stood and grabbed the rope. The rest was easy. Ki only had to climb a few hands up the rope and he was at the loft opening. It was dim, and musty with the odor of moldy hay, and the samurai could see nothing as he slipped silently into the loft, then dropped flat.

Ki took a deep breath and waited a couple of minutes for his eyes to adjust to the poor light. As they did, he realized that the loft was divided by thick beams running up to the roof, as well as a latticework of crisscrossing rafters. Although Ki's vision was exceptional, he could not see his quarry and decided that the man was probably hiding behind one of the many support beams.

Ki reached into a vest pocket and removed a *shuriken* throwing star. Staying low and avoiding the thin blades of slanting sunlight that cut through the gloom, Ki moved forward. He could see the ladder opening in the floor and knew that his man was somewhere very close.

Suddenly, the ladder rattled. Ki knew in an instant that Dustin was shaking it to distract the hidden gunmen, and the ruse worked. A silhouette emerged over the opening and Ki saw the flame of a gunshot blossom from the assassin's weapon.

"Drop it!" the samurai shouted through the darkness, the dust, and the cobwebs.

The gambler whirled and began to fire blindly. Ki's arm shot forward; his star blade flashed through a thick slab of sunlight, then vanished into darkness on its deadly path. When it struck the gambler in the forehead, Ki heard the familiar sound of blade burying itself into bone.

The gambler staggered and squeezed off a last bullet into the floor, then he crashed forward. He struck the ladder, then toppled through the hole. Ki heard the ladder rungs breaking like giant matchsticks all the way down.

Ki expelled a deep breath and walked over to the hole in the loft floor. He squatted on his haunches and peered down at the gambler's body. Dustin stepped into view. The wounded man used the tip of his boot to roll the gambler over onto his back. He stared at the *shuriken* blade buried in the gambler's skull, then cocked his head back and gazed up at the samurai.

"What the hell is that damn thing? Some kind of a knife, or something?"

"It's a star blade," Ki explained.

"A *what*?"

"Never mind," Ki said, stepping back and heading out to the rope and the pulley. In less than a minute he was back on the ground and ordering Dustin to remount and ride back into town to see Dr. Branch.

"You all go along," Dustin called back to them. "I'll catch up with you by tomorrow."

"You sure?" Ki asked.

"Hell, yes! Main thing is to get Ed back to the ranch. I'll be along soon enough."

"All right." Ki turned to the three new hands. "Let's get out of here before we have to answer too many questions."

The three new cowboys seemed to think that was an excellent idea. They waited until Ki jumped back onto the wagon and took up the lines.

Ed raised his head and stuck up a note that read: DID YOU GET THE MURDERIN' BASTARD?

"Yeah," Ki said, "Dustin killed the one that jumped you and I killed another, a gambler."

Ed balled up his note and scribbled another. AIN'T THAT DUSTIN HELL ON WHEELS!

Ki turned back to the horses and gave them a sharp slap on the rump with his lines. When they were under way, Ki said to his friend, "Dustin is a piece of work, all right."

★

Chapter 8

Dustin finally caught up with Ki and the cowboys when they were within ten miles of the Circle Star Ranch's outer boundaries.

"My horse, Charlie, is a bit stiff, too," Dustin explained in the way of an excuse. "The doc stitched him up good before I let him have a look at me."

"How noble," Ki said. "And how is your wound?"

"Doin' just fine, thank you. The doc said I needed at least a day's rest. Lilly said I needed a lot more than rest." Dustin winked. "Anyway, I stayed in bed for about thirty-six hours and did my best to ease their concerns."

Lester, upon overhearing this, barked a ribald laugh, and so did the other cowboys. Lester said, "I'm just surprised that you didn't bring Lilly along!"

"Naw," Dustin said. "I wouldn't want to embarrass Miss Starbuck with the likes of that poor girl. Lilly has a good heart and she sure knows how to satisfy a man, but she ain't exactly genteel company. Know what I mean?"

The Amarillo cowboys knew and they got a big

chuckle out of Dustin's delicate way of putting such an obvious difference between the famed Jessica Starbuck and a woman like Lilly.

As they traveled along, Dustin learned that the Circle Star Ranch had more than five thousand head of cattle and a payroll that exceeded that of most towns. It had everything you could expect from a big ranching empire, even a small company store where supplies and tack could be purchased at cost. And when their wagon finally topped a low rise and they could see the ranch headquarters, all the Amarillo cowboys were impressed.

"We're almost home, Boss!" Dustin shouted down at poor Ed Wright, who hadn't made so much as a sound during the long ride south, although it was clear that he had suffered a great deal.

When they drove into the ranch yard, Jessie and some of the cowboys who were working on some corral fences hurried over to greet Ki and the newcomers.

"Jessie," Ki said, "I'm afraid that Ed has been hurt."

Jessie rushed over to the wagon; when she saw her foreman's face all swollen and discolored, she bit her lower lip and grabbed the edge of the wagon bed. "How bad is it?" she asked Ed.

He picked up his pad and pencil. BROKEN JAW AND CRACKED RIBS. BE FINE IN A WEEK OR TWO AND READY FOR THE ROUNDUP.

Jessie whirled to face Ki. "I can see that he wasn't kicked in the face by a horse or stomped by a bronc. So what happened?"

"He was attacked," Ki said. "A big man jumped him in the dark. Ed never had a chance to defend himself."

"I want that man sent to jail." Jessie's voice was tight with anger.

59

"I'm afraid I already killed him," Dustin said, stepping down from his horse and removing his Stetson. "Miss Starbuck, my name is Dustin. I whipped the fella that beat up your foreman and then I shot off . . . well, I killed him when he and another fella ambushed us on our way out of town."

Jessie turned to face the tall, handsome young cowboy with the sandy hair and dark blue eyes. "You say you killed him?"

"I did. Ki shot the other one. They were a real bad pair. I'm sure everybody in Amarillo figures good riddance to their passing."

Jessie looked back at Ki. "Let's get Ed into the house and a bed. I'll send for our own doctor and then we'd better have a good long talk, just the three of us."

Ki nodded.

"Whatever you say, Miss Starbuck," Dustin said, replacing his hat. "But first, I'll give you a hand with your foreman. He's a real tough old bird, and I know that he wouldn't mind me saying that."

"Ed *is* tough," Jessie said. "He's been ramrodding Circle Star for many, many years. I'd be lost without him."

"All the more reason I'm glad I was there to save his bacon when it counted," Dustin said cheerfully.

When he moved away to help carry Ed into the house, Jessie pulled Ki aside. "Who *is* that man?"

"I don't know," Ki replied. "He's sort of a mystery. But I can tell you this—he's cocky and very dangerous. I don't know what it is about him, but I have my doubts."

"But he did save Ed, didn't he?"

"Oh, yes," Ki said. "I consider myself completely at fault for letting Ed go out to recruit cowboys without me. I would have insisted on going along, only I sensed that Ed felt a little more comfortable by himself. You know how some men take a strange notion of people who don't look or dress like themselves."

"Yes," Jessie said, "I do."

She hurried after the cowboys as they carried Ed into her house and into a big, spacious spare bedroom that had plenty of morning light and a window that looked out toward the corrals, tack room, livery, and blacksmith.

"There," Jessie said when Ed was resting on the bed. "You've lost some weight and you look tired. We're going to remedy that with steaks and . . . oh, my, you can't chew anything, can you."

Ed scribbled: NOPE. BUT I AM STARVING.

"Then we'll make some of the best soup you ever tasted. Rich as Midas. Can you handle that?"

Ed nodded vigorously.

"Good," Jessie said with relief. "Would you like a bath?"

BATH AND A BOTTLE OF WHISKEY.

Jessie looked into the pain-filled eyes and nodded. Ed wasn't much of a drinker, so she knew he was in real pain when a bottle of whiskey was one of his first requests.

"You'll have the best of both," she promised. Jessie leaned forward. "That man named Dustin, did you hire him?"

A nod.

"Is he a top hand?"

MAYBE. MAYBE NOT. GOOD MAN WHO KNOWS CATTLE. HE'S A KEEPER, MISS STARBUCK. SAVED MY LIFE.

"Well," Jessie said, "that's enough for me. We'll put

him on the payroll. I see you hired three other men, and they look to be good hands."

DUSTIN HIRED THEM FOR ME.

Jessie's eyebrows raised. "He did?"

YEP. I TRUST HIM. YOU CAN, TOO.

Jessie frowned. "Ki has second thoughts about the man. And you know he has a pretty keen insight into people."

KI IS WRONG ABOUT DUSTIN.

"Well, since we are indebted to the man for helping you, I'm willing to give him the benefit of the doubt. He seems engaging and earnest enough. I hope that he'll prove to be an excellent cowboy and employee. I'll have a word with him shortly."

Ed nodded and tried to smile but it was so pathetic that Jessie really wished he hadn't bothered. The poor man's face was just a mass of swelling and bruises, the kind that started out black and blue and then began to take on a sort of unhealthy yellowish cast after a few days.

"I'll be back after you've had a bath," she said. "I'm going to have Conchita help you with that."

Ed managed to shake his head.

"It's all right," Jessie said. "Conchita is over sixty years old and she's seen everything there is to see. Besides," she added, trying to tease and raise her foreman's spirits, "Conchita has always had a little crush on you Ed. You know that."

Somehow, Ed blushed. Jessie patted his hand and left the room.

Ten minutes later, she was seated in her father's library with Ki and Dustin.

"Dustin, before anything else, I want to say how much

gratitude I feel toward you for helping Ed," Jessie said. "He is simply irreplaceable."

Dustin sat up a little straighter. Jessie judged him to be about six three, with a full head of hair, strong features and a magnificent set of shoulders.

"Miss Starbuck," Dustin said, "I consider it an honor to have been able to right a great wrong. I just wish that I'd anticipated them going after your foreman instead of myself. You see, I'm really the man that should have been waylaid. Ed, he didn't do much. It was me that called their bluff and exposed the gambler for being a liar and a cheat."

"Well," Jessie said, "that's all water under the bridge. And frankly, if you've just come along as a good Samaritan, I'd like to offer a little cash as a token of my appreciation."

"Oh, no, ma'am!" Dustin said, waving his hands, palms out. "I didn't ride all the way down here to collect money. I came because Ed asked me to sign on for your roundup. And . . . to be honest, just to see if you were really as beautiful as I've heard you were."

Jessie felt her cheeks warm. She didn't know quite what to say, but he did.

"And you are, Miss Starbuck. You're the most beautiful woman I've ever had the pleasure of laying eyes on—and I've been to a few big cities on both coasts, so I've seen some lovely ladies. But you definitely top them all."

"Thank you," Jessie whispered, embarrassed because she knew that her cheeks were coloring.

"Miss Starbuck, do you mind if I tell you that I'm not going to be your top hand?"

"What?"

"Well," Dustin began, "I haven't cowboyed for a couple of years, so I'm probably a little rusty. Now, them other three boys that I hired over in Amarillo, they're the real deal. The best, unless I'm badly mistaken. They've ridden for all the big outfits in Texas, and I can tell that they're going to turn out to be top hands. But I might struggle a little and disappoint you. I'll try not to, but I might."

Jessie didn't quite know how to respond to his level of candor. In truth, she would have hired Dustin and found a job for him on her ranch even if he'd never ridden a horse in his life. After all, he'd risked his skin to save Ed.

"I am," Dustin began, "more partial to good horseflesh than I am to cows."

"Are you a bronc buster?"

He grinned. "I can ride the rough-string better than most. But I'm not one to break horses with a quirt and a pair of big-roweled Spanish spurs. Nope. I'd rather take a good young horse, one that hasn't been mistreated or taught bad habits, and show him kindness and patience. I believe that the best horses are not broken, but gentled."

Jessie grinned, too. "Mr . . . what *is* your last name?"

He hesitated, and his eyes dropped to his big hands, which held his Stetson in his lap. "I'd rather just let my past stay in the past. Names don't mean much anyway, do they? It's what a man is and does that matters, isn't it?"

"That's true," Jessie said. "But I have to be careful about whom I employ for a lot of reasons. I can't hire a killer or a wanted man, no matter how much I might feel in his debt."

"I've killed men," Dustin confessed. "More than I

64

care to think about. But I've never pulled a gun out of hate, anger, or greed. I've killed for love and in self-defense. I've killed cheats, murderers, and outlaws."

"What about the law?"

"You mean, why didn't I get the local marshal to handle that kind?" he asked.

"That's right," Ki said. "Obviously, a person has the right to defend themselves, but beyond that . . ."

Dustin didn't look to the samurai. "The law is written straight and sets up the rules. But the men that are called to carry out those rules are just men, and some of them are as bad as the outlaws they're supposed to arrest and bring to trial. Sometimes, a person just has no choice but to be his own judge and jury."

"And then an executioner?" Jessie asked, slightly unnerved by this man's matter-of-fact attitude toward killing.

"That's right," Dustin said. "Ki and I both killed men in Amarillo just three days ago when we could have ridden on out of town and let them live. They tried to ambush us, but missed. So what should we have done?"

"Gone to the marshal and had them arrested," Jessie flatly stated.

"And then what? Gotten stranded in Amarillo for a few weeks or even months until a jury could finally be chosen and brought to a verdict? A verdict that would have resulted in nothing more than a slap on the wrist? A few months of jail time, maybe?"

Dustin ran his long, slender fingers through his hair. "Miss Starbuck, I'm not rich or smart like you. I'm just an ordinary fella, but I do know that justice would not have been served if we hadn't sent those two men to the cemetery. And I believe in my heart that they'd killed before and would have killed again if we hadn't done what needed to be done."

Jessie looked to Ki, who said nothing. She came to her feet. "I can't argue that point because I don't know all the facts of the matter. And perhaps you're right. In fact, I expect you *are* right. But if we, as individuals, become the law unto ourselves, then our society is simply one ruled by the strong. Justice becomes who is the strongest, and might becomes right. And, Dustin, that just won't do."

"Yes, ma'am," he said, coming to his feet. "Now, if there's nothing else that you need, I reckon I'll go see if I can find an empty bed in the bunkhouse and try and make myself useful before it's time to eat."

"I'd like you to work with the horses," Jessie said quickly. "I like what you had to say about breaking them with kindness and keeping their spirit. It's the principle I've instructed my bronc buster to use, but it's one that he has yet to learn to appreciate."

"Sure," Dustin said, "I know the type. It's a lot easier and faster to fight a bronc and whip him into submission than it is to spend time earning a green horse's respect and trust."

"I agree," Jessie said. "My bronc buster's name is Mike Halverson. He hasn't worked here very long and he's not easy to be around, but do what you can."

"I will," Dustin said. "I can get along with most anyone if they're reasonable."

Jessie watched Dustin walk away and felt compelled to follow him out of the library and out the front porch. "Dustin?"

He turned. "Yes, Miss Starbuck?"

"I don't know what you're hiding from me about your past. I'm just going to make it a point not to ask again. The only thing I *do* ask is that your past does not intrude upon the harmony and smooth working relationships that exist on Circle Star."

"They won't, Miss Starbuck. If I thought I was bringing you trouble, I'd never have come."

"You . . . you seem a little stiff. I guess that you really haven't been in the saddle much lately."

"I've been in the saddle," he said with a boyish grin that she didn't quite understand. "But the reason I'm stiff is that a bullet grazed me when that fella I killed got in his first shot. But it won't slow me down any. I'll still be able to do a day's work."

"When the doctor arrives, I want to make sure that we have a look at that bullet wound. Is it serious?"

"No."

Jessie hesitated, then took Dustin's hand. "Come into the kitchen and let's have a look."

"It can wait for the doctor, Miss Starbuck."

"I'll be the judge of that," she said, practically dragging him back into the house, up the hall, and into her kitchen.

"Take off that shirt and sit on that stool," she ordered.

He removed his shirt, and Jessie saw that he was well proportioned. His muscles were flat and firm. A bandage was taped under his arm, and when Jessie gently peeled it off, she saw that Dustin had sustained a nasty flesh wound, which was already starting to fester.

"This needs to be cleaned and packed with medicine right away," she said, calling for Conchita to bring some of the water that she was already heating for Ed.

"It'll wait for your doctor," Dustin said.

"I don't think so," Jessie replied, leaning close, brow furrowing with worry. "I'll do it."

His arm encircled her waist.

"Hey!" she protested, trying to pull away but finding that his arm was like a steel band holding her in place. "What are you doing?"

"I was wondering if there was anything you *couldn't* do," he said with a smile as he released her.

Jessie tried to look angry at him but guessed she wasn't doing a very good job. "And?"

"And," he said, "since you couldn't pull away from me just now, it's nice to know that you're human just like the rest of us."

Looking into his handsome face, Jessie felt her heart pound faster. "Dustin, you'll find that I'm *very* human. But I'm also your boss."

"Yes, ma'am," he said, lust burning through his striking blue eyes.

★

Chapter 9

Dustin found a bunk and was stowing his gear when a cowboy in his thirties, short and bowlegged, came in and greeted the newcomers.

"My name is Scottie," he said by way of introduction. "Glad to see you men. We were looking at some long hours during roundup, shorthanded as we were. You boys will make a big difference."

Dustin, Lester, and the other new men gave their names and shook hands all around. Scottie said, "We don't wear sidearms on the ranch because there's no need. So pack your guns in your bedrolls and come on outside. I'll introduce you around and show you the layout of the place."

Dustin hadn't thought about the fact that none of the cowboys were packing guns. He'd completely forgotten that they were unnecessary on a big ranch, many of which had similar policies to prevent the crew from getting into arguments that could turn fatal.

"That's a mighty fancy rig," Lester said when Dustin

unbuckled his holster and rolled his cartridge belt around his six-gun. "Awful fancy for a cowboy to wear."

Dustin shrugged. "Some men wear fancy boots, I just happen to favor a fancy gun and holster."

"You, uh, you pretty good with it?"

"Fair to middlin'," Dustin drawled. "You know, good enough to shoot what I aim for."

"Most of us cowboys aren't that good a shot," Lester said. "Never enough money to waste on practice bullets."

"I don't consider practicing a waste," Dustin said.

Lester just shrugged. "We better get outside," he said.

Scottie introduced them around. When one of the Circle Star cowboys asked Dustin for his last name, he dodged the question by saying, "Dustin is all I go by. You sing it out, and I guarantee I'll answer."

That seemed to satisfy the Circle Star cowboys, although a few of them couldn't help but give him rather curious looks. But mainly they were very friendly, since they had quickly learned about the role he'd played helping their highly popular foreman in Amarillo.

Scottie waited until everyone had met and then he said in a loud voice, "I'm going to be foreman until Ed gets back on his feet, and I don't expect to change a thing. We've a roundup coming up, that means all of you need to be checking up on your gear and your string of horses. Get the horses shod and get your saddles, tack, and ropes oiled and ready for work. I expect that every man will have at least four horses to use during the roundup and they need to be in top condition."

"We're a couple short," one cowboy said. "And will the new men be expected to use their own animals?"

"They might have to," Scottie said. "It depends on

how that new band of broncs we just bought turn out."

"They'll be ready to ride in time for the roundup," Halverson vowed. "They won't be broke rope horses or know much, but they'll get a man to where he's going. They're all young and tough."

"Tough from you beatin' the hell outta them," another cowboy said under his breath. "The poor horses act like whipped dogs with their tails stuck between their legs."

Halverson was a tall, rawboned man with red hair, red skin, freckles, and a peeling nose. He walked with a limp, and his arms seemed excessively long. He chewed Mugwump tobacco, which was the worst kind of poison that a man could lay his hands on and call tobacco.

Spitting a big stream of Mugwump on the ground, he squinted and studied the cowboys. "Which one of you bastids said that?"

"What?" a cowboy asked innocently.

"That I beat on the broncs so's to make 'em act cowed."

"Hell, I dunno," the man who'd made the remark said. "I guess somebody musta said it, but I ain't sure who."

"You bastids talk outta the sides of your damn mouths and you ain't got no balls to speak of, either."

Dustin felt the cowboys chill. A moment ago, they'd been having a little fun with Halverson, but now the thing had turned ugly with his insult.

Scottie must have felt the sudden antagonism because he stepped in to head off trouble. "Now, Mike," he said, "let's just drop the whole damn thing and remember that we're all working to the same end—and that's to get things ready for another successful roundup. We had a mild winter, lots of spring rain, and plenty of good grass. The cattle ought to be fat and healthy, so let's

71

just count our blessings and pray that the cattle prices are high this fall."

"Don't much matter," Halverson said. "Miss Starbuck is so rich that every last cow on this ranch could die tomorrow and it wouldn't hurt her as much as it would us to miss a single damned payday."

Dustin couldn't help himself from saying, "That sure is shitty attitude, Mike. If you ride for the brand, it seems to me that you ought to try and make it money even if it already does have money."

"Who the hell asked you for your worthless advice?" Halverson snarled, turning to glare at Dustin. "You just got here and you don't know jack-shit!"

"I know a pure son of a bitch when I see and hear one," Dustin said with a smile that had no warmth.

Halverson stiffened. Like a dog, the hackles seemed to rise on his neck and he leaned forward, jabbing a dirty finger at Dustin. "I ain't of a mind to listen to no smart-assed advice from a dandy boy like you."

"Mike!" Scottie snapped. "That's about enough of that kind of talk."

But Halverson wasn't paying any attention to Scottie. His pale blue eyes studied Dustin, and then he spat a stream of Mugwump that struck the earth between Dustin's boots, spattering them with a vile, yellowish-brown liquid.

"I'm gonna teach a few things that ain't even got to do with broncs," he hissed.

"You aren't going to teach me anything," Dustin said. "Unless it's how to be a complete and perfect asshole."

Halverson's cheeks flamed bright red. His hands, which were big and covered with scabs, knotted; he would have attacked if Scottie and several of the other

72

cowboys hadn't stepped into his path.

A few minutes later, on the way to the dining hall, Scottie moved up beside Dustin and said, "You made yourself a bad enemy. Mike might look dumb and clumsy, but he's as strong as an ox and can hit like a Missouri mule. He's whipped two of the men and got most of the others buffaloed."

"He messes with me," Dustin warned, "and I'll make sure that the only thing that so-called bronc buster ever attempts to mount again is a toilet seat."

Scottie burst out laughing. "What are you going to do, kick his ass clean off?"

"Something like that."

"Well," Scottie said, "I should warn you that Miss Starbuck has a rule about fighting, and it's a hard one. She'll fire both men involved, no matter who started the fight."

"Oh, yeah? And what if a man is just defending himself?"

"I don't know," Scottie said with a frown, "but that might make a difference."

"I'd hope so," Dustin said. "Miss Starbuck is smart enough to know that no man worth his salt is going to be humiliated by someone like Halverson just to hold his job."

"Come on." Scottie pushed Dustin into the dining room, which was nothing but a long table and cookstove at one end. "Maybe I'll talk to Miss Starbuck and tell her that it'd be better if you worked somewhere else rather than with Mike and those new broncs."

"I wish you wouldn't do that. I really wouldn't be too happy to be working anywhere else but with the new horses; in fact, I might just up and quit."

"I'm just trying to help you out," Scottie said.

"Thanks, but I like to help myself out," Dustin replied. "Most of the grief in my life has come when other people thought that they knew what was best for me."

Scottie blinked, but then he nodded. "Suit yourself," he said as he walked away.

Later, as the sun went down, the cowboys gathered outside the bunkhouse, and a couple of them played guitars and harmonicas. Most of the men sang old cowboy songs, and even though Lester chided Dustin in a good-natured way to sing along, Dustin declined. He was watching the ranch house because he could see the slender silhouette of Jessica Starbuck as she moved from room to room.

Dustin couldn't get over the rich woman's beauty. He could still smell the scent of her body and felt his maleness enlarge as he thought of how her waist had felt when he'd pulled her up close. In her unguarded moment of surprise, he'd seen Jessie's alarm and anger, but also her sexual excitement before she'd ordered him to release her.

Yes, Dustin thought, *the day will come, and it won't be long before I'm sleeping up there in her bed and listening to these cowboy songs coming through the pretty boss's bedroom window.*

And once that happened, Dustin figured his life would never be the same.

★

Chapter 10

The next morning, Dustin headed for the breaking corral determined to avoid any kind of confrontation with Mike Halverson, although he suspected that was no longer a possibility. The previous night, Dustin had pretended not to notice the hateful glares that he kept receiving from the Circle Star bronc buster. The man wasn't likely to forget or forgive that Dustin had made him look like a fool.

That was the trouble with life, Dustin decided. A man needed the company of other men and certainly the sweet association of women, but relationships were difficult to keep in balance. One wrong word, one misunderstanding, and everything was blown sky-high. Dustin had learned that hard lesson from his late father.

Major Gideon Gamble had been a man whose behavior was completely unpredictable from one day to the next. He'd been a Civil War hero, decorated many times over. He'd survived and even flourished during the war and returned to Texas with a passel of followers to settle near the Rio Grande. He'd built a cattle ranch and made it profitable, but he'd lived life recklessly: his favorite pastime was raiding into Mexico to steal horses and cattle.

Gideon Gamble had become a legendary figure, a man who might have become the president of the fledgling Republic of Texas if not for his mercurial temperament and his uncanny ability with a six-gun. He'd fathered six children, but Dustin was the only legitimate one; the others had been the forgotten bastard offspring of Gideon's unions with saucy Mexican wenches.

A brief and violent stint as a Texas Ranger had served only to enhance Gideon's reputation as the most dangerous and violent man on the Rio Grande. Dustin had once seen his father shoot down three armed men in a gun battle that had lasted nearly four minutes and expended more than a hundred bullets. True, all parties had been roaring drunk, but in the end, it was Gideon Gamble who'd been the lone man standing—and that only because he'd switched to a Bowie knife when he'd run out of ammunition.

People still talked about Gideon in the same awed tone of voice used when they uttered the name of the devil or a saint. But in the end, Gideon's legions of enemies had teamed up to gun him down in Laredo. And fearing that his fifteen-year-old legitimate son would one day seek retribution, they'd tried to eliminate Dustin, too.

They'd killed Dustin's mother, but by luck and the pluck of an old Mexican woman named Juanita, the boy had been spirited away. He'd changed his name and moved to Arizona, keeping his father's gun, which he'd finally worn out in practicing for the day when he returned to Laredo and evened the score. When he'd probably die just like his father—who had almost come to believe he was as immortal as his own legend.

From the time that Dustin was able to walk, his father had taught him that the only law that *really* mattered was the law of survival. And from everything that Dustin had seen during his life, he continued to believe this was true. That was why he had never ceased to practice with a gun and knife and had perfected his killing skills until he was confident that he would never be taken down unless it was by a force equal to the killing of a Texas legend.

But now, almost nine years later, Dustin had still not gone back to even the score in Laredo. Why? He couldn't be sure. Perhaps it was because he remembered watching his father's body being riddled with bullets and then being urinated upon by his cowardly enemies. Or maybe it was the way they butchered his mother. Dustin didn't know. All he knew was that he had not mastered an unreasoning fear of the men who had slaughtered his parents. And until he could face them, he would just keep on working and getting ever more deadly until he was confident that he would be man enough to do the job. A job that even his father hadn't been able to do.

"Hey, you bastid!" Halverson shouted. "You gonna stand there all day with your thumb up your ass, or are you gonna show me how to bust a bronc!"

Dustin tore free of the vivid and recurring nightmare of the blast from a ten-gauge shotgun that had almost ripped off Gideon Gamble's famous face. Dustin shook himself and wiped his clammy hands on his pants. As usual when in the grip of that horrible memory, he was sweating profusely, and his heart was beating as hard as if he'd been running up a mountainside.

Dustin went over to the round breaking pen where Halverson had a roan gelding snubbed down to a thick post.

"You want this son of a bitch?" Halverson challenged.

"Go ahead," Dustin replied, climbing up on the top rail to watch. "You started him, you finish him."

"You bet I will," Halverson vowed. "You watch how it's gonna be done around here, mister."

Dustin suspected that he already knew how it was going to be done. Halverson was just a bronc buster, the same kind that he'd seen on dozens of ranches while cowboying around West Texas and Arizona.

Two men jumped at the roan's head, one pulling a towel over its eyes while the other froze the roan in pain by biting its ear. Dustin could see the gelding quivering with a mixture of fear and anger.

"Watch me!" Halverson shouted. He swung into the saddle and yelled, "Turn 'im loose, boys!"

The two cowboys faded back, and the gelding shook its head as if in a daze.

"Yah!" Halverson shouted, driving his big-roweled spurs into the roan's flanks so viciously that hair and hide peeled away and Dustin could see blood run. "Buck, you jug-headed bastid!"

The roan was smallish and more frightened than angry. It tried to buck and that seemed to excite Halverson, who spurred it furiously. The bronc buster had wrapped his reins around his saddle horn to keep the roan from dropping its head so that it couldn't get any power into its bucking.

It was no contest. Mike Halverson ripped open the

roan's flanks like a wildcat's claws could open up the snout of a foolish hunting dog.

"The asshole's locked his spurs," Dustin heard himself shout. "That's what he's done. He's locked his goddamn spurs!"

"That's Mike's way," one of the cowboys said. "Mike says if they don't roll, he can get a bigger bite on the bark."

"Of course, he can! Look how he's tearing up that roan's flanks!"

Dustin didn't even realize he was leaping off the corral fence. One minute he was sitting there watching the sorry spectacle of a man punishing a horse for no damned reason except orneriness and the very next he was scrambling across the pen and leaping up into the air and grabbing Halverson by the shirt.

"Hey!" Halverson shouted. "You crazy sumbitch!"

Dustin pulled the bronc buster off his horse, and they fell hard. The roan, freed from its tormentor and finally able to get its head down, began to buck like something mindless.

Halverson was strong, tough, and a vicious fighter. Once on his feet, he went for Dustin; only instead of looping an overhand as Dustin expected, he kicked for the crotch. The kick was hard and fast and Dustin couldn't get completely out of its way. The blow caught him in the hip and was so painful that he staggered, and thought his hip had been broken. While he was trying to recover, Halverson threw a series of wicked punches that rocked Dustin and then dropped him in the dirt.

The fight would have been over right then if the roan hadn't come bucking between them, almost stomping Dustin in its crazed frenzy. A swinging stirrup caught

Halverson in the eyebrow and opened him to the bone. Halverson swore and batted blood from his eyes. He surged forward with every intention of kicking Dustin's face in, but the blood fouled his vision and caused him to miss.

Dustin came to his feet and caught Halverson's upraised leg. With a mighty heave, he threw the leg at the sky and sent Halverson crashing down on his back. Dustin booted the fallen man in the ribs and Halverson screamed and doubled up. Dustin kicked him again and sent him rolling under the bucking horse.

"Get up!" Dustin raged.

Halverson did get up, but not straight. He swayed forward and his hand reached behind his back.

"He's got a knife!" one of the cowboys yelled. "Look out!"

Dustin also had a knife at his belt, and he yanked it out. It was his father's Bowie, and it was perfectly balanced in his hand.

"You want to get carved up, come on!" Dustin urged. "But if you want to live, I'll let you go."

Halverson's lips pulled back from his teeth. "Pretty boy, when I'm done carving up your face, the sight of you is gonna make the wimmen sick!"

They began to circle, but the damned roan kept charging in between them, bucking and squealing. Once, Halverson took a swipe at the animal and laid open a deep gash across its haunches. The next time that the crazy bronc passed between them, Dustin attacked. He went in with his blade held low, cutting edge up. He thrust for Halverson's throat, felt his parry being blocked, then kicked out. He felt his boot strike Halverson in the thigh and saw the man stagger.

Dustin waited, growing more and more confident that his opponent was not quick and was in such pain that he could not fully concentrate or react. This was proved a moment later when Halverson attacked, knife coming in low and then slicing upward.

Dustin twisted his wrist and his blade scored deep just behind Halverson's thumb, cutting all the way down to the bone. Halverson moaned and his eyes widened with panic. The knife in his hand started to slip away, so he switched it to his left.

"Still time to get out of here alive," Dustin panted, circling, looking for one last opening. "Still time to turn tail and run while you've got blood in your veins."

"Bastid!" Halverson screamed, feigning a thrust in the desperate hope that Dustin would commit himself and lose his balance.

It was a fool's hope: Dustin merely stepped back with a wolfish grin on his lips. "Not very good, Mike. Not good at all."

The bronc buster choked with fury and despair and then threw himself forward, knife cutting upward. Dustin's blade came down at the same instant, and it scored first. The two biggest fingers of Halverson's left hand were cleanly severed in one neat swipe. Even before the scream could escape the bronc buster's mouth, Dustin whipped his blade in a backhand motion across the man's throat, opening it wide.

Halverson's mutilated hands fluttered to his neck and feebly attempted to close the gaping wound. His face turned as pale as chalk, and his eyes bugged up at the vast Texas sky.

Dustin turned away. He saw the two cowboys staring at him with fear and horror and knew that they had never seen a real knife fight before and were shocked almost witless by its savage butchery. Dustin heard the bronc buster's throat gurgle and heard the man choke and hiss for air that would not come because he was drowning in his own blood.

Halverson struck the rails and pitched halfway through them, already more dead than alive.

"Holy Jeezus!" one of the cowboys managed to gasp.

"Catch up the roan," Dustin ordered.

"Huh?"

"Catch up the roan!"

The two cowboys snapped out of their reverie and jumped for the horse. In a few moments, they had its lead rope. When one of them started to blindfold the animal, Dustin said, "No!"

He went up to the roan and began talking to it in a low, soothing voice that helped calm his own rattled nerves. Dustin knew the roan was wild with fear caused by pain and the scent of blood—its own and the dying bronc buster's.

"I'm taking him out of the corral," Dustin announced, wiping clean his father's blade with his bandanna, and then sheathing the Bowie. "Open the damned gate."

The taller of the two jumped for the gate and had it open in a flash. Dustin swung into the saddle and turned the roan's head toward the opening. The horse shot forward, certain it was running for freedom. Dustin found his stirrups and gave the animal its head. He let it run across the yard and out onto the range. After a mile or so, the horse began to slow. Dustin forced it to run on and on until it was ready to drop. Finally, he reined the horse in, knowing it had no strength left to fight.

Dustin twisted around in his saddle and gazed back at

the ranch. He suspected that when Miss Starbuck found out the way he'd killed her bronc buster, even though the man had started the fight, she would have no choice but to fire him. At worst, he might be taken to some jail and held for trial.

"Another squandered opportunity," he said bitterly.

He plow-reined the roan this way and that. It shivered with exertion and fear, and Dustin knew that it must be in great pain from the big cuts in its flanks.

"I had to give him a taste of his own damned medicine, didn't I?" he asked the roan.

The roan bobbed its head. Dustin relaxed. He could see a spring up near a low hill where there were cottonwood trees and grass.

"Let's give them some time back there to think this thing out," Dustin decided, reining the bronc toward the distant spring. "Maybe they'll just fire me, and I can ride away without anymore fuss or trouble."

They moved slowly toward the spring. It was already growing warm, and Dustin hoped he'd find that the water was sweet and cool.

Later, he'd ride back. He'd doctor the roan's flanks with grease to ward off the flies, and then he'd pack his saddlebags and bedroll and be on his way.

Chapter 11

When Jessica heard the front door slam, she looked up from the production report of her mining company in South Africa. Scattered all across her desk were figures and reports from other companies she owned that she needed to study.

"Miss Starbuck!"

It was Scottie, and from the look on his face, Jessie knew at once that something terrible had happened. "What's wrong?"

"There was a fight," Scottie said. "An awful fight between Mike Halverson and that new fella that we just hired on in Amarillo."

"Dustin?"

"That's right."

"How bad did Mike hurt him?"

Scottie brushed a shaky hand across his eyes as if he wanted to erase the sight he'd just seen. "It ain't the new man that got hurt," he said. "It was Mike."

"Tell me everything," Jessie ordered, getting up from

84

her desk and walking over to her father's bar, where she poured Scottie a stiff drink. "Just relax and tell it to me slow."

Scottie tossed the drink down. "Mind if I have one more before I start?"

"Help yourself," Jessie said, her anxiety increasing because Scottie was not normally a man who was easily shaken.

"All right, Miss Starbuck," Scottie said, "I might as well give it to you straight. Mike is dead."

Jessie took a sharp breath, then whispered, "How did it happen?"

"They were both in the breaking pen, and Mike was showing off on that handsome little roan gelding with the bald face that we figured might make a fine woman's horse. Anyway, Mike got a little carried away and the next thing everyone knew, that Dustin fella was leaping off the fence and dragging Mike clean outta the saddle."

"I see."

" 'Course, Mike went pretty much loco. You know what kind of a temper he had."

"A nasty one," Jessie said. "I probably should have fired him before now. Did he hurt the roan?"

"Damn right he did, Miss Starbuck! He'd locked his spurs and ripped that poor bugger's flanks wide open."

"And this Dustin . . . did what?"

"They went to fighting. You won't believe it and neither would I except that a couple of our boys were watchin', but Dustin whipped Mike! Anyway," Scottie continued, "Mike got whipped real bad and that's when he pulled a knife. This Dustin fella, he had one of his own. A big Bowie. I reckon that Mike should have figured out right then and there that it would have been

85

better to just run up the white flag, but he didn't."

Jessie leaned forward. "So they had a knife fight, right in our breaking corral?"

"That's right! I was in the barn and most all the boys were setting fence posts out by that back corral, so we had no idea what was happening. But I guess it was a terrible fight."

"Dear heavens," Jessie whispered, reaching for the decanter of brandy and pouring herself a glass.

"The boys that was there said they never seen anything so bloody in their lives. And when the cuttin' was done, Mike was missing two fingers and . . . and his throat was slit open from ear to ear."

Jessie sat back down at her desk. She emptied her glass and took a deep breath. "Then what happened?"

"This Dustin fella told the boys to catch up that roan. When they did, Dustin walked up to it speaking so nice and low that you'd have thought he was a preacher who just delivered a sermon on love instead of a cold-blooded knife fighter. Anyway, he mounted the roan and it didn't buck or nothing."

"He just slit open Mike's throat and then calmly rode the bronc?"

"Well," Scottie said, "not exactly. The roan was smellin' blood. That corral is . . . well, never mind. But the roan was pretty spooked so Dustin climbed on board."

"And then what happened?"

"Dustin said to the boys, 'Open the damned gate.' Just as cool as ice he did. Just 'Open the damned gate.' "

"And they did."

"Of course they did! Then Dustin went racing away."

"Where?"

"I don't know. None of us thought it would be too healthy to follow that crazy man."

Jessie refilled both their glasses, and they drank in silence for a moment before she said, "But Mike was the one that pulled the knife first, right?"

"Why, sure, but he was all cut up and he'd been beaten when Dustin cut his throat!"

"Mike would never have stopped over a couple of fingers," Jessie heard herself say. "He was too proud to lose, and he'd won too often to believe that he could be defeated."

Scottie stared. "Miss Starbuck, are you saying that—"

"I'm saying that Mike needed to be stopped from ruining that horse, and Dustin did what had to be done."

Jessie walked over to a hat rack and took her Stetson. "And as for the fight, if Mike Halverson was the first to pull a knife, then anything that happened afterward was obviously a matter of self-defense."

"But . . ."

Jessie's voice sharpened. "You knew Mike. After he'd been whipped in front of our cowboys, do you really believe he would have let Dustin live? To watch the man that whipped him every day? Of course not! Mike *had* to win, always. He was the kind of man that would rather die than lose."

"Yeah," Scottie said, rubbing his hand across his face, "that's the truth. None of the boys would even gamble with him. He whipped hell out of the only one who beat him at cards."

"You never told me that."

"I didn't hear about it until last week. Happened at a line camp. The cowboy what got whipped just rode away and never came in to collect his pay."

"Well," Jessie said, "that only supports what I've just told you."

"You want us to bury him in the regular cemetery?"

"No," Jessie said quickly, "he doesn't belong with my mother and father. I'll have his body taken to his family in Overton."

"They've got a bad reputation and they're going to be damned upset."

"I know, but that can't be helped."

"What about Dustin?"

"I'm going to go have a talk with him."

"You'd better take the samurai along."

"No," Jessie said, "I want to talk to him in private. Go ask the men if they saw which direction he was heading. Have Sun saddled; I'll be out in a few minutes."

"I sure don't think much of this idea," Scottie said. "If he was up and about, Ed would have a fit."

"I don't think it serves any useful purpose for Ed to be upset. Besides, this Dustin doesn't strike me as the kind of man who would harm a woman or an innocent person. He defended himself, Scottie. Just as anyone would do under the circumstances."

"I don't know about that," Scottie said. "Like I said, the boys that were watching off the corral fence said that Dustin could have walked away from that fight after he cut Mike's fingers off and had him bleeding like a stuck hog. But he didn't walk away. He cut Mike's throat."

Jessie shook her head lest the vision of that terrible scene penetrated her brain. "Just . . . just get my horse saddled and point me in the right direction. Dustin's bags and his gun belt are still in the bunkhouse, aren't they?"

"Why, sure."

"He's not the kind of man who would leave those things behind and run," she said. "I need to find and talk to him before I make any decisions."

"You need to fire him, Miss Starbuck. We'll tie his bedroll and his bag on the horse he rode down here from Amarillo. There's no need for the man to come back. Not after what he did to Mike, there isn't."

"All right," Jessie said. "Saddle his horse and tie his gear down."

Scottie looked relieved. "He came here lookin' like a pretty nice fella. I guess you just can't judge a book by its cover, huh, Miss Starbuck."

"Often not."

"Well," Scottie said, "I tell you, nobody liked Mike Halverson, but they'll be spooked about this killing for a long time. That Dustin fella would never have been trusted after what he did to Mike. He's just . . . just too damned *different!*"

Jessie nodded. She'd sensed right away that the tall, handsome young stranger from Amarillo who had saved Ed Wright's life was very different. He had seemed remote and aloof. At the same time, she had sensed a deep sadness that ran through the man and had made him seem extremely vulnerable under the hard facade that he used for protection.

Minutes later, when Jessie came striding out of her ranch house, Ki was waiting on the porch.

"I want to go with you to find the man. Either that, or allow me to go bring him back."

"I doubt you could," Jessie said. "At least, not alive. I'm afraid, that he wouldn't listen to another man, Ki. But I can talk to him. Then I'll decide whether or not to invite him back to the Circle Star."

"You'd do that?"

"I might."

"But . . . why?"

Jessie really didn't have an answer—at least, one that made great sense. "I just need to hear his side of the story," she said. "I feel that I ought to give him at least that much of the benefit of the doubt because he saved Ed's life. Don't you agree?"

"I guess I do," Ki said after a long moment of reflection. "I just don't want anything to happen to you, that's all."

"It won't," Jessie assured her friend. "I promise."

Ki nodded, but he still looked very worried. And maybe, Jessie thought, he had every right to be.

★

Chapter 12

Jessie had no trouble spotting Dustin. It was obvious that the man was making no attempt to run or to hide. He was, in fact, doing quite the opposite. His shirt was off and he had washed in the little pool of spring water and then stretched out on the grass, staring up at the sky with his fingers laced behind his head.

When he heard Jessie's horse, he rolled over onto his side and watched her with apparent unconcern. In fact, he looked so peaceful and calm that Jessie could scarcely believe that this same, boyishly handsome young man had actually slit another man's throat.

"I was daydreaming," Dustin confessed with a wide grin. "I was dreamin' that you came out here alone to see me instead of jumping to all the wrong conclusions and storming out here with your boys bent on taking me to some jail."

Jessie dismounted and tied her horse up beside the roan. She inspected the bronc's flanks and was appalled at the damage that Mike had inflicted with his cruel spurs.

"Why didn't you fire him?" Dustin asked, his smile slipping. "How could you have kept a man like that on your payroll?"

"It was an oversight," Jessie admitted. "And one that I'm not very happy about. It just . . . it happened."

"He was one of the cruelest bronc busters I've ever come across," Dustin said, sitting up.

The man was long and lean and tanned, which led Jessie to suspect that sunning himself out on a prairie or range was something that this strange man from Amarillo enjoyed on a regular basis. But in spite of the tan, she could see awful bruises and welts where Mike Halverson's fists had marked his flesh.

"Did you really have to slit his throat?" she asked in a voice that held a tremor.

"I could have let him live," Dustin admitted. "I could have gotten out of that corral alive."

"Then . . ."

"But he would have tried to kill me the first time I turned my back on him and I couldn't take the chance that he might have succeeded." Dustin shook his head. "My father made that mistake."

"Letting his enemies live to fight again?"

"Exactly. The very men that he showed mercy to ganged up and shot both him and my mother down."

"Where?"

Dustin's eyes had a pained, faraway look. He whispered, "It doesn't matter, does it?"

"I guess not." Jessie sat down next to the man. "What was his name?"

92

It was a long time before Dustin spoke. So long, in fact, that Jessie was beginning to wonder if the man had even heard her question. But finally, he said, "My father was Major Gideon Rutherford Gamble. Maybe you've heard the name."

Jessie's jaw dropped. When she recovered enough to speak, she said, "I've not only heard his name, I've heard his legends. At one time, he was said to be the most dangerous man in Texas."

"I expect that he was," Dustin said. "All I know was that he killed a lot of men, but the ones that he showed mercy to tricked him and shot him down. Then they killed my mother and tried to kill me."

"But, why?"

His eyes misted. "I guess they must have known that my father taught me how to fight back. How to use a gun, a knife, or my fists. And I guess they figured that someday I'd get big and strong enough to go after every last accursed one of 'em."

"But you didn't." It wasn't a question because she could see the answer by the look on his face.

"Not yet," he said. "But I'm going to, someday soon. I just . . . well, I just hate to go back there and kill all those men."

"How many?"

He frowned. "There were six in on it. One died and another is in prison for life. So that leaves four."

"I remember hearing about the Gamble boy when I was just a little girl. I didn't believe the story."

"You should have, because I'm that boy and the story was true. I've pretty much been on the run ever since." He looked right into Jessie's eyes. "You see, I was the only surviving witness to those murders. And although I

93

doubt anyone would take the word of a boy, they know that they need to put an end to me if they are to sleep well at night."

"They came after you?"

"Hell, yes!" Dustin lowered his voice. "I'm sorry. But yeah, they came. Not them, actually, but men they hired. Real bad men. I've been hunted like a rabid dog for years. That's why I don't go by my full name."

"Why did you tell me this story?"

He plucked a blade of grass and chewed it thoughtfully. "I guess I figured that, since you hired me and since I got to thinking I might even stay through your roundup, I owed you something."

Jessie leaned closer. "You don't owe me. I owe *you* for saving Ed."

"You paid me back with a job," Dustin said, eyes burning into hers.

"It wasn't enough."

"Maybe you'd like to pay me back with something other than money," he said, gaze dropping boldly to the shape of her breasts pressing against the restricting fabric of her blouse.

"What do you mean?" Jessie asked, knowing exactly what he meant.

"I mean this," he said, leaning over and kissing her mouth as he drew her to his warm, brown skin.

Jessie resisted for about ten seconds, and then she gave in knowing that she wanted this young man as badly as he wanted her. In less than a minute, he had her blouse open and his tongue was laving her full and aching breasts. Jessie moaned, a soft sound deep in her throat like the purring of a giant cat. She took his head in her hands and moved his mouth from one breast to the other until she felt her body tingle with pleasure and desire.

"This is wonderful," she breathed, unbuttoning his pants and slipping her hand down until she held his already throbbing shaft.

He pulled his pants off, and she gasped at the size of him. Jessie felt her own pants being unbuttoned; she could hardly wait until she had this man inside of her. His skin seemed to burn from the sun and his desire, and her breathing was already coming fast.

"Hurry," she begged. "I want you inside me!"

In the urgency of their need, they tore off the rest of their clothing. He was all over her, kissing and touching and making her writhe with pleasure. The bronc snorted and rolled its eyes, but Jessie scarcely noticed as she spread herself wide so that Dustin could have her completely.

Without interrupting the attention he was lavishing on her breasts, Dustin put a hand under each of Jessie's knees and lifted her, spreading her thighs as he plunged his big rod into her hot, wet depths.

"Oh, honey," she panted. "You feel so good!"

Dustin threw his head back, arched his back and laughed at the clear blue sky as he began to thrust into Jessie. He cradled her soft buttocks in his hands holding her suspended and to his will while she moaned with pleasure, staring up at his bronzed torso. With every powerful thrust of his hips, he would jerk her buttocks hard at the end of each delicious stroke. Jessie thought she might go mad before he had his way with her.

"Faster, please," she begged, "faster, or I'll go insane before you finish!"

"No, you won't," he promised, leaning forward over

95

her and planting his hands beside her shoulders as his body plunged in and out, in and out. "You're *made* to do this, Miss Starbuck. Never was a woman's body made more perfectly to be taken by a man."

Jessie's head rolled from side to side. He kept lifting and plunging until her very blood seemed to burn with need. "Hurry," she begged. "Please, hurry!"

He dropped her buttocks to the earth and fell on her like a starving animal. Now he began to drive even deeper into her body until she felt battered and almost dazed. But when he slowed a little and pulled back, she gripped him even more tightly and whimpered, "Don't stop, don't pull up!"

"I'm ready," he panted. "Are you?"

"Oh, yes!"

His hard, hot body seemed to melt into her own, and he took her with all his strength. She clutched at his neck and an ecstatic scream filled her throat as lights exploded like Chinese rockets and she felt the fire of his seed flood her womb.

Jessie went limp, and Dustin collapsed on her. For a long time, they lay trying to get their breath, each so in union with the other that it was impossible to tell how much or how little they were physically and spiritually joined.

Finally, he rolled off and lay on his back, lacing his fingers behind his head, just as she had seen him do when she'd ridden up a lifetime ago.

"Dustin," she said, her voice sounding foreign. "I'm not sure what happened to us."

"I am." He chuckled. "We were perfect together. In a very short while, we'll be perfect again."

She snuggled up closer to him, hands moving over his

hard muscles and the rise and fall of his chest. "We can't just lie out here and make love all afternoon."

"Of course we can," he said, turning toward her with a look of amusement. "You *own* all this. You can do whatever you want on it."

"Yes," she said, happily. "But what if . . ."

"They won't come. At least, not for awhile."

"I can't be seen in this state. I'm their employer!"

He laughed. "Yes," he said, "I can see your point. All right, we'll get my bedroll and go make love behind that big tree and our horses. We'll have plenty of time to see anyone coming and get dressed."

"All right," she said, marveling at her acquiescence.

"What's going to happen when they come?" he asked. "Are you going to have them arrest me, or am I fired?"

"None of that," she told him. "I'm going to have to figure a way so that we can do this as often as possible."

"And what about Halverson?"

Jessie's smile faded. "It was a fair fight. You defended yourself."

"And that's all?"

"Yes," she said. "That's all."

"Things are going to be different here from now on, Miss Starbuck."

"Jessie."

"No, I want to keep it Miss Starbuck so I don't forget in front of your men."

"I guess that would be better." Jessie drew in a deep breath. "After you leave, where will you go?"

"I don't know."

"Will you ride south to avenge your father and mother?"

"Probably."

"I wish you wouldn't." Jessie hugged his neck. "Dustin, revenge and hatred are terrible things. They corrode a human heart. You need to let go of them."

He was quiet for several minutes. Then he said, "I will, Miss Starbuck. Just as soon as I've killed those four men, I promise you that I will."

It was not what Jessie wanted to hear, but she knew better than to lecture him or else he would simply leave. She had her purpose in life; right now, he saw his as that of getting even.

Jessie studied his bruised face. "Halverson was vicious and tough, wasn't he."

"Yes," Dustin said, "he was both. One of the toughest men I've had to fight in quite some time. He would have been a terrible enemy and probably would have found a way to bushwack and kill me some night."

"I'm glad that he's dead instead of you," Jessie said. "But you can't kill anyone else."

"Only if they won't leave me alone," he promised. And after a moment he added, "Will that samurai of yours leave me alone, Jessie?"

The question chilled Jessie. She pressed close to Dustin and said, "Yes, he will. The only reason he'd ever fight you would be to save me."

"Then we'll never have to fight," Dustin said, "because I'd never hurt you, Miss Starbuck. In fact, I'd give my life to save yours."

"I believe you."

Dustin raised up and studied her breasts. "They are works of art," he decided out loud. "And I'm never going to get enough of them in one measly afternoon."

Jessie arched toward him as his mouth closed first

98

over one nipple, then the other. "I don't know when we'll have this chance again," she breathed. "So let's just get as much of each other as we can."

He nodded and slid onto her body and pushed between her legs, and it was then that Jessie realized that he was already long and hard again.

★

Chapter 13

Jessie and Dustin returned to ranch headquarters at dusk. When they rode in, Ki, Scottie, and most of the Circle Star cowboys were anxiously waiting. Jessie, her skin sunburned and her body feeling as if it had been kneaded like bread dough, nevertheless possessed an inner glow that only the samurai detected.

"By gawd, Miss Starbuck," Scottie said, hurrying over to take care of her horse. "We were damned worried. I was about to lead a search party to look for you."

"Dustin rode quite a ways," Jessie said, "and we needed to have a good long talk."

Before dismounting, Jessie turned to her crew and said, "What happened today in the breaking corral is a tragedy. Mike Halverson went after Dustin, who had no choice but to defend himself. I want all of you men to put it behind you, but also to remember that I won't tolerate fighting. If someone can't get along, he'll be fired."

Scottie frowned. "But . . ."

100

"That's all," Jessie said, loudly. "We should be able to start the roundup by next Tuesday, and I want every man to be ready for a long, hard month's work."

The cowboys nodded. Jessie watched Dustin untie his bedroll and warbag. When he turned and headed back to the bunk house, the cowboys parted in his path. Jessie knew that Dustin would never really be a part of this crew now. He was just too intense and too self-possessed, too full of the need to avenge his parents. Sooner rather than later, Jessie knew the young man would turn his horse south toward the Rio Grande.

Dustin stopped at the door of the bunkhouse. He turned and gazed back at Jessie as she strode toward her big ranch house. At the front porch, Jessie paused and turned, and her green eyes reached out to Dustin.

He smiled, confident that she was going to miss him as much as he was going to miss her tonight. Then he stepped into the bunk house and said to a very young cowboy that was nursing a broken arm, "Was Mike Halverson's bunk a top or a bottom?"

The cowboy started and swallowed nervously. "Bottom. Mike made sure that he had the best of everything around here."

"Where did he sleep?"

"Right over there," the kid said, pointing. "But Scottie took that bunk and . . ."

"And he can take another," Dustin said. "Because now I'm the toughest son of a bitch on the payroll. I'm meaner than a wet badger and about as hard to handle as a Texas tornado. Do you believe that?"

"Why, I guess there is."

"Maybe you're a little smarter than you look," Dustin said to the kid as he tossed Scottie's gear aside and threw his own onto the bunk. "I already forgot your name."

"Ted. Ted Cotton."

"Well, Ted, this outfit has a new bronc buster, only I don't break broncs, I gentle them. There's a difference, you know."

"Yes, sir!"

"How old are you?"

"Sixteen."

"I haven't broke my arm yet, but I broke a leg when I was your age."

"You did?"

"Yep. A bucking bronc that turned out to be an outlaw drove me into a fence. The toe of my boot got hung up in the fence; when the bronc bucked away from it, he almost ripped my right leg clean off."

"My, oh, my."

"Broke it in four places," Dustin said. "How many breaks in your arm, Ted Cotton?"

"Just one, but the doctor said—"

"Then you ought to be on your feet and moving," Dustin interrupted. "Tell me this much, Ted. Do you like horses, or cattle?"

"Both."

"I'll need an assistant. That pair of cowboys that eared and put the blinders on the roan this morning aren't to my liking. I want you to help me starting tomorrow."

"But the doctor said I wasn't to be using this broke arm until it was all healed."

"You won't have to use it, you can help me one-handed," Dustin said, "starting first thing in the morning. Hell, maybe I can even teach you a thing or two about how to train a wild horse to ride and drive."

"Yes, sir!"

"I'm not a sir. My name is . . . is just Dustin. Not sir."

"Yes . . . Dustin."

"Good."

They both heard the cook shout that it was time to eat. Dustin scowled; his belly felt as hollow as a dried gourd. "You hungry, Ted?"

"I dunno."

"Well," Dustin said, "you'd better eat up, because they'll be no pussy-footing around tomorrow when we start working with that rough stock. You can't be weak and making mistakes. Most of those horses aren't mean, but there are always exceptions to the rule. We can't be taking any chances when our lives are at stake, now, can we?"

Ted shook his head. "But . . . but what can I do with only one arm?"

"You can hold a rope, untie a gate latch, lead a skittish horse, check to make sure that a cinch is tight. You can do all sorts of things."

"I guess I can at that." The kid managed a smile, then blurted, "How come you cut Mike's throat and killed him?"

Dustin stiffened. He momentarily wavered between slapping the kid or just telling him the truth. Truth won out this time.

"Halverson was rotten to the core," Dustin said. "He liked hurting men and horses. And he was a killer, same as me. But I never liked to hurt anyone. It's just that I've had to do it in order to stay on top. It's like riding a horse. A man sometimes has to use a little spur, a flick of the quirt. But a good man never uses more force than is necessary to get the job accomplished.

103

Halverson used as much force and pain as he could get away with. Finally, it caught up with him."

"They say . . ."

The kid's eyes dropped to his lap.

"What do they say?" Dustin asked, needing to get it all out on the table.

"They say that you cut off his fingers."

"I did," Dustin said. "One of the first rules of knife-fighting is to disarm your opponent so he can't kill you. You can either cut his arm, hoping to slice the tendons, or you can try to whack off his hand at the wrist, or sometimes just his fingers so he can't hold a grip."

The kid looked fascinated but also a little aghast. "You're a knife fighter?"

"I'm a *fighter* when I need to be. I can be others things, too," he added, thinking of how he'd spent the afternoon making love to the rich and beautiful Jessica Starbuck. "We all are different things at different times."

"You're good with broncs, too, aren't you?" Ted asked.

"Yes," Dustin said, "I take pride in that work."

The kid was warming up, growing bolder. They were alone and he was going to be Dustin's assistant, and that made him feel that he could skirt around some dangerous boundaries.

"Do you take pride in killing?"

"No!" Dustin lowered his voice. "That's a dumb question, and I'll not tolerate any more like it. What I feel about killing is my own business, and I keep it to myself. Suffice to say that I'd rather not kill anybody, but I won't leave an enemy behind that'll one day try and kill me."

"Mike would have shot you down sooner or later," Cotton said. "I know that."

"I knew it, too," Dustin said. "Let's go eat before it's all gone."

Ted climbed out of his bunk and followed Dustin out of the bunkhouse as they went to join the other cowboys.

When Dustin stepped inside the cook shack, all conversation died. The cowboys turned to stare at him. When the silence became uncomfortable, Dustin decided that it needed to be addressed.

"All right," he said to all of them, "I know that you're wondering who and what I am. Well, I'm going to try and be top hand on the roundup next week. And before that, I'm going to break and train some horses so we'll have some new horseflesh to ride out during the roundup." He looked around. "Any more questions?"

"Just one," Scottie said.

"And that is?"

"What are you going to do about Mike Halverson's kinfolk when they come looking to kill you?"

This was the first Dustin had heard about any kinfolk. "I don't plan to worry about it until they come. I've found that most of life's worries never even happen."

"This'll happen. Mike has three brothers. When they hear about how you cut his throat, they'll want to cut you up into pieces."

"I acted in self-defense."

"They won't care."

"In that case," Dustin said, "I'll have to kill them, too. And don't worry, I won't expect anyone to help."

Scottie nodded and set down, his expression wintery. "It's just that we're only cowboys, not gun- or knife-fighters."

"Sure," Dustin said as he went to fill his plate.

★
Chapter 14

Ed Wright was extremely upset the next morning as Jessie prepared to set out to deliver Mike Halverson's body to his family down near Jackknife, some thirty miles southwest of the Circle Star Ranch.

Ed scribbled a note to Jessie that read: DON'T GO TO THE HALVERSON PLACE. THOSE PEOPLE AREN'T TO BE TRUSTED.

"I know," Jessie said. She had never been to the Halverson place, but she'd heard troubling stories about it. It was reputed to be a mean little horse ranch where Oliver Halverson had a brood of ornery sons. Everyone had said that Mike was the best of the lot, and even he hadn't been much good. "Ki is going with me," she added.

TAKE AT LEAST A DOZEN MEN!

"I can't do that," Jessie said. "There's too much work to be done around here."

THEN AT LEAST TAKE A FEW. MISS STARBUCK, THOSE MEN ARE VERY DANGEROUS!

Jessie had learned to trust her foreman's opinions, so she nodded. "All right," she agreed. "I'll take a few men along, but I doubt that they'll be needed. It was a fair fight, Ed, and that's exactly what I'll tell the Halversons."

THEY WON'T BELIEVE YOU.

Jessie frowned. "All right, then, I'll also take along the two cowboys who were helping Mike and saw the whole thing. I can't do any more than that."

ARM YOURSELF WITH SHOTGUNS.

Jessie forced a smile. "You sure know how to cheer a girl up, Ed. Now, come on! I know that family has a bad reputation, but they're still people. I'm sure that they knew Mike well enough to believe that he went down fighting."

Ed shook his head, his brow deeply furrowed with worry. He wrote, TAKE SHOTGUNS!

"We will," Jessie said. "I promise."

Jessie met Ki on the porch and told him Ed's concerns. "He's pretty upset. I promised to take a half-dozen men with shotguns. I also told Ed that I would take along John and Pete, the two men who had been helping Mike yesterday afternoon when the fight started."

"This family sounds like trouble."

"I know, but even as mean as he was, Mike still deserves to be buried on their land. So we've really no choice in this matter."

Ki didn't look a bit pleased as Jessie sent for Scottie and told him what she wanted. Before turning to get the men, Scottie said, "I want to come along. I know Ollie Halverson. I wouldn't say we're exactly old friends, but he might listen more kindly to a familiar face."

"Maybe so," Jessie said. "All right."

"Thanks," Scottie said. "There is one other thing."

"And that is?"

"I think if we're all armed to the teeth with shotguns, it'll just provoke that bunch. Make 'em think we're guilty as sin. I think we all ought to have guns, just not make any big show of force."

"Are you sure?"

"That's just my opinion, Miss Starbuck. I knew that family pretty well because I was raised only about six miles from their place."

Jessie considered this for a moment and then said, "Since you know them, we'll do as you suggest."

Scottie nodded. "I can't say as how I'm looking forward to seeing that family again, but I will feel better coming along than I would have staying here and worrying about you."

"How many Halverson men *are* there?"

"There's hardly any way to keep track; I doubt that even old Ollie himself knows. There's cousins and uncles and shirtsleeve relatives all over that part of Texas. They don't even recognize themselves, sometimes; I've heard stories of one cousin shooting another to death not even realizing they were blood."

"I'm beginning to get the picture," Jessie said.

"Well, it ain't a pretty picture, I'll tell you for sure. The Halverson clan is hated all over that part of the country."

"Then we *are* in for a difficult time," Jessie said. "Well, Mike needs to be buried—the sooner the better."

When Dustin saw Jessie and the large body of horsemen emerge from the barn, he forgot about the buckskin mare he was about to gentle and came across the yard.

"Miss Starbuck," he said, "where are you and all these men going?"

"To a town called Overton, out to the Halverson ranch," Jessie said. "We're returning Mike's body to his family."

Dustin looked around at all the heavily armed men and felt a stirring of alarm. It sure didn't take *that* many men to deliver a corpse.

"It appears you're expecting trouble. Trouble on account of me."

"You were attacked and had every right to defend yourself."

"Then why . . ."

Jessie didn't want to sound impatient, but neither did she want to seem familiar enough with Dustin to argue with him in front of her crew.

"We just need to make sure that there's no trouble, Dustin. Now, you've got plenty of rough stock to break, so get to it."

"Take me along," Dustin said, trying to keep his voice calm. "I mean, if there's going to be trouble, I ought to be a part of it."

"I quite disagree. The Halverson clan will want to know the full circumstances of Mike's death. If you were there, it would be like adding salt to the wound. So, that's why we're going and you're staying."

"But . . ."

Jessie's eyes turned icy. "That's an order."

Dustin stiffened. He was not a man to take orders from anyone—but, under the circumstances, he could see that Jessie might have a good point in insisting that he remain behind.

"All right," he managed to say.

Jessie couldn't hide her relief. "We'll be back late tomorrow night," she said before she and Ki drove away in the buckboard with Scottie and the other cowboys she had chosen following right behind.

Dustin watched the party until they grew dim on the horizon. Then he went back into the breaking corral and snapped angrily, "Ted, let's get this mare saddled and broke."

"But I thought we were just going to tie her up to the snubbing post and let her get acquainted with us today."

"A change of plans," Dustin said impatiently. "I'm thinking I might not have as much time as I thought."

Dustin saddled the frightened mare and, as he began to talk to her and rub her sweaty coat in order to sooth her nerves, his own impatience and anger melted away. An hour later, he did step into the saddle, but only to sit quietly and talk to the trembling mare, rubbing her neck all the while and speaking in the easiest voice possible.

"Why," Ted said when Dustin stepped down and slowly began to unsaddle the mare, "she didn't even buck or nothing."

"Tomorrow I'll actually ride her around in the pen for an hour," Dustin promised, "and she won't buck even once. You'll see. And by the end of this week, she'll be as gentle as a pet dog wanting to please."

"You've sure got a way with horses," Ted told him, eyes filled with admiration.

Dustin winked. "If you think I'm good with horses, you ought to see me with the ladies."

Young Ted laughed and said, "My arm feels a whole lot better today."

"I doubt that," Dustin said. "The difference between

today and yesterday is that your mind is on honest work instead of fretting about that broken bone. When you don't think about an injury so much, you most generally find it doesn't hurt."

"I guess that must be the way of it," Ted said, nodding in ready agreement. "Do you expect that Miss Starbuck, Ki, Scottie, and the boys have delivered Mike's body to his family by now?"

"I don't know," Dustin said. "But I sure wish that I had gone along with 'em."

"You probably should have," Ted agreed. "Ki is a fighter, but Scottie and the rest can't even hit the side of a barn door with their six-guns."

"Not very many cowboys have the money or interest to practice and learn how to shoot straight," Dustin said, his eyes fixed on a distant point to the south. "And if they did, there'd be a whole lot more dead men coming out of the saloons every day and every night."

"Where'd you learn to shoot so good?"

"My father taught me."

"Would you teach me how to shoot and use a knife?"

Dustin's attention was pulled back to the kid. Ted Cotton was as innocent as a lamb, but eager to lose that innocence. "Kid," Dustin said, "I'm going to teach you how to gentle wild horses and make them into the best cowboy ponies that they can be. And that's *all* I'm going to teach you."

Ted looked hurt but Dustin didn't care. Sometimes, the more innocent a man was, the better chance he had of staying out of trouble and living to a ripe and respectable old age.

They heard the cook shout that it was time to eat, but Dustin realized that he really had very little appetite.

He was thinking that, after everyone went in to eat, he might saddle old Charlie and ride down to Overton to make sure that everything was working out peaceably for Jessie and her boys. Not that he meant to disobey orders. Not really. The truth of the matter was that he could claim that he'd gone looking for his horse or some damned story. Probably no one would even notice his absence tomorrow, except for Ted Cotton.

"Hey, Ted," he called. "I'm going to take a little ride tonight."

"Where to? Want me to come along?"

"No," Dustin said, "that wouldn't be much to my lady's liking."

Ted blushed. "Oh."

"And just in case I'm not back tomorrow morning, you get that buckskin mare out and re-saddle her. Climb into the saddle and just rub her neck for an hour or two, then unsaddle her and turn her back into the corral. Then get another and do the same."

"But what if . . ."

"You'll do just fine," Dustin assured the young man. "I could tell yesterday that my first impression of you was right."

"It was?"

"Yep. You're a natural with horses. Same as me."

"I am?" Ted appeared ready to burst with boyish pride.

"You are," Dustin assured the kid, who was suddenly looking mighty pleased with himself. "And if you go slow, one day you'll make a fine horse trainer."

"Why . . . why thank you very much for your confidence!"

"It's deserved," Dustin said, clapping Ted on the

112

shoulder. "Now you just do as I say, and if anyone asks where I've gone, you tell 'em that I went to see a friend."

"Can I tell 'em it's a *lady* friend?"

"Sure." Dustin laughed. "Why the hell not!"

★

Chapter 15

Jessie and her men took rooms that night in Overton, but they would have been about as comfortable sleeping on the prairie. Overton wasn't much, just one rattletrap hotel, two saloons, a livery, and a general store. Overton was really nothing more than a little ranching community supported by a number of large cattle ranches and a bunch of smaller ones like the one owned by the Halverson clan.

"If you've got Mike's body, I'd just dump it here and skedaddle!" the hotelman told Jessie. "And then I'd try and put as many miles between me and those Halverson men as I could before they find out what happened to Mike. By the way, how'd he get it?"

Jessie had anticipated the question and framed an answer that would not be as inflammatory as if she'd said that Mike's throat had been cut from ear to ear.

"He was killed in a knife fight," Jessie said.

"Musta been a dilly," the hotelman said, "because I saw Mike carve a Mexican up one night and he was about as good with a sticker as they come."

"Well," Jessie said, not wishing to prolong this conversation, "Mike attacked one of my men, and that was his big mistake."

"Don't expect Ollie to buy that," the hotelman said. "He never could stand the idea of one of his boys getting bested. He taught every last one of 'em how to fight and shoot."

"Apparently, not well enough," Jessie said, feeling even more pessimistic than before.

"I still say you ought to just dump Mike's body in front of the livery and make tracks back to your ranch."

"We're not the kind to leave unfinished business," Jessie said. "I feel an obligation to let his family know what happened and to extend my condolences."

"Ollie Halverson ain't going to accept no apologies," the hotelman said. "Mike was one of his favorites, and he's going to want to get even."

Jessie remembered that dire prediction when she went to her room and tried to sleep that night. She saw no reason to tell Ki or her cowboys until tomorrow that everyone who knew this awful Halverson clan expected them to seek revenge.

Just before dawn, she heard a tap-tapping on her window. She was awake instantly and reached for her pistol, knowing she had only to call out and Ki would be at hand to help. But most likely, she thought, the intruder outside was some drunk who hoped that she might want to invite him into her bed.

"Go away!" she whispered. "Before I have you shot!"

Dustin's familiar chuckle brought Jessie to her feet. When she raised her window, the man hopped inside and took her into his arms.

"Are you crazy?" Jessie exclaimed. "I *ordered* you to stay at the ranch!"

"I know," Dustin said, "and I forgive you."

"You forgive . . ."

"You just didn't realize that I'm a complete failure at taking orders."

"Dustin," she said in exasperation as she pulled away from him, "I gave you my reasons. Your coming here will serve no good purpose."

"Sure it will," he said. "At the very least, we can spend an hour or two making love this morning."

"You're crazy!"

"Am I?" Dustin picked her up and carried her back to bed. In a few moments, while Jessie's heart began to quicken, he'd undressed and joined her. She was furious with him for disobeying her orders, but when he began to kiss her breasts and mouth, she was swept away with passion.

"Dammit," she panted as he mounted her and their hips began to move in a love circle, "what am I going to do with you?"

"You're doing just fine right now," he said, his hard manhood causing Jessie to moan with pleasure. "And as for the Halversons, we can face them together and take things one step at a time."

Jessie supposed that he was right. She *hoped* that he was right. The only thing that she really knew for certain was that she was suddenly incapable of anything except making love to this wild, handsome, and very dangerous young man.

"Feeling better?" he asked as their bodies began to move with increasing urgency.

"Much, much better!"

Dustin growled low in his throat and then he took her quickly to a place that felt so good even angels would have wept with envy.

Jessie fell asleep, sated with pleasure. When she awakened, Dustin was gone, but he'd left a note by her bedside that read: NOT WISHING TO COUNTER THE BOSS' ORDERS, I'VE VANISHED BUT I'LL BE CLOSE TODAY IF NEEDED. AND IF NOT, I'LL SEE YOU BACK AT THE RANCH.

Jessie was pleased. She would not have been able to have concocted anything approaching a good reason why Dustin had joined them in the middle of the night despite her stern orders.

She dressed quickly and met her men for breakfast in an empty room of the hotel. The meal was surprisingly good: bacon, eggs, and sourdough biscuits. Jessie was famished and wondered if anyone noticed the whisker burns on her cheeks or her slightly bruised lips. Dustin was a powerful lover, but he did leave his marks on a woman.

"Have a good night's sleep?" Scottie asked.

"Yes, I did."

Ki looked up from his meal, and his dark eyes seemed to read right through Jessie's facade. And later, when they went out to get their horses, the samurai confirmed that he knew about Dustin when he said, "Where did he go?"

"I'm not sure," Jessie whispered. "He said he'd keep out of sight unless he was needed."

"That would be a very good idea," Ki said. "I just hope he doesn't change his mind."

117

"He won't."

"How can you be sure of anything that man says or does?" Ki asked. "So far, he's proven only one thing—that he answers to no one and fears no one. I'm not sure that he's to be trusted about anything, Jessie."

"Let's get the wagon hitched."

The samurai opened his mouth to speak, then changed his mind. Without another word, he went to help Scottie with the wagon. Mike Halverson's corpse was getting riper by the minute.

"Get that body in the damned ground before everyone gets sick!" the liveryman groused. "Why don't you just dig a hole and be done with it!"

Jessie didn't bother to answer. She and her men had come this far; they would finish this miserable business because returning a body to its family was the right and proper thing to do.

"All right," she told her men when the wagon was hitched and they were all mounted. "We're going to show force, but act sorry as hell about Mike. We don't want any trouble, but if it's clear that trouble has to happen, then I expect you men to make your shots count. I'll be damned if we're going to allow them to get the drop on us. Is that clearly understood?"

Scottie and the cowboys nodded. Ki just climbed up on the wagon and raised the lines to indicate that the talking was over and that it was time to go.

Jessie joined the samurai. No words were exchanged between them, but she knew that Ki was extremely troubled. His bow and quiver of arrows was close at his side, and Jessie knew that he carried *shuriken* star blades, which were as deadly as bullets in his skilled hands.

"Maybe it will be all right and we'll have no trouble at all," she said to Ki.

"Maybe," he replied, but the grim tone of his voice made a mockery of his words.

★

Chapter 16

"We're on Halverson land now," Scottie said as they splashed through a shallow stream and followed a rutted wagon road that lead straight as an arrow out from Overton. "Their ranch house is about a mile up that stream. You can't see it because its hidden in all those cottonwood trees."

Jessie studied the few thin cattle she saw grazing. "Looks like they've overgrazed their range."

"They're a real hardscrabble bunch," Scottie said. "There's little doubt that they're cattle rustlers and horsethieves."

"Then why hasn't the law put a stop to them?" Ki asked.

"They *kill* the law, that's why," Scottie said. "At least, they did when I was growing up. Murdered three marshals. Of course, they did it on the sly so that there were no witnesses, but everyone knew that Ollie Halverson was behind the ambushings. Overton's last marshal was a joke. A common drunk that sobered up only long enough to collect a few dollars from the Halversons so that he could drink some more."

Jessie shook her head. "I don't understand how this kind of thing goes on today," she said. "This isn't a republic anymore, it's a *state*. We have laws."

"Laws aren't worth the paper they're written upon if they can't be enforced," Scottie said. "And in this county, Ollie Halverson *is* the law."

"That will change before long," Jessie said. "And if the county can't manage this outlaw family, then the state or the federal government will step in and take over."

"Maybe," Scottie said, "but right now, we need to worry about delivering Mike's body, and getting the hell off this ranch in one piece."

"We will," Ki promised.

Jessie glanced aside at the samurai and was glad that he was with them. Ki wouldn't say a word if things went along peaceably, but if there were trouble, he would be a force to be reckoned with. And somewhere behind them, or maybe even ahead in the line of cottonwoods that marched toward the Halverson ranch house, Dustin would be waiting in case the bullets started to fly. And finally, Jessie had a strong body of loyal cowboys who would fight to the death, if necessary. Admittedly, they weren't gunfighters, but they were capable and would not break and run if the fight turned against them.

"They've spotted us," Scottie said.

Jessie could see the Halverson ranch now, just bits and pieces of it through the cottonwood trees. Perhaps a dozen or more men were gathering in the yard and there was a lot of activity.

"They already look stirred up," Jessie said, trying to hide her own mounting anxiety. "And there's a lot of them."

"We're outnumbered," Ki said.

Jessie hadn't expected to see so many. Usually, most of the working men on a ranch would be out on their range during the day and only a few yard hands, cooks and injured cowboys would be hanging around during the morning. Apparently, things were much different here.

"My advice is to just go in slow and easy," Scottie said. "You and Ki roll that wagon into the yard and just tell 'em what happened, say we're damned sorry about Mike getting killed, then ride out."

The closer to the ranch yard they got, the more Jessie was beginning to think that she should have taken the hotelman's advice and just dumped off Mike's body to be claimed by his family. The Halversons were massing like a swarm of hornets—and their stingers were Winchester rifles.

"I'll do the talking," Jessie said.

"Might be better if I did," Scottie suggested. "They know me, and they don't have much respect for women."

"That's *their* problem," Jessie said in a terse voice.

"Far enough!" a tall, full-bearded and barefooted man shouted, lifting the barrel of his rifle. "State your business!"

Ki pulled the buckboard wagon in and the cowboys reined up their horses. They were about fifty yards from the Halverson clan, too far to carry on a conversation without shouting, but close enough to say what was necessary.

122

"My name is Jessica Starbuck. I own the Circle Star Ranch just north of—"

"We heard of you. What do you want?"

"Mike Halverson was my bronc buster," Jessie yelled. "He was killed and we're returning his body."

The tall man visibly stiffened. Then he turned aside and yelled over his shoulder, "Pa, the woman says Mike is dead!"

"I heard her!" came a roar from the dilapidated ranch house. "I heard her, but I damn sure ain't heard why!"

Oliver Halverson emerged from his house. The man was immense. Six-five, at least, with a huge, protruding gut and a wild mass of gray hair and beard. His movements were ponderous, even shuffling. He wore only a pair of patched bib overalls, no shoes.

"Woman," he bellowed, coming forward while his family fell in behind, "what happened to my favorite boy?"

"He was killed."

"By *what*, gawdammit!" Halverson thundered. "By animal, by man, by what!"

Jessie took a deep breath. She knew she was well protected, but the huge old goat advancing on her was so repellent and intimidating that she was frightened.

"He was killed in a knife fight," Scottie blurted. "You remember me, don'tcha? Scottie Johnson. My folks had a spread over by the—"

"Shut up!"

Scottie's voice died as if he'd been dropped from a hangman's scaffold. Jessie's anger flared high enough to smother her fear. "I won't stand for you talking to my men like that! Although it certainly wasn't necessary, we came to deliver your son's body for burial."

123

"You want thanks?" the old man hissed, eyes narrowing to slits. "You bring me the body of my favorite boy, and you expect my thanks?"

"I expect nothing," Jessie said, "other than for you and your family to remove Mike's body from this wagon so that we can turn around and go back home."

The old man's face went from white to crimson, and his fat hands lifted to signal his clan to spread out on both sides. Jessie felt her palms turn clammy and she felt Ki shifting his weight in preparation for trouble. She couldn't be sure what Scottie and her men were doing, but she would have bet anything that they were sweating bullets.

"Jethro!"

"Yes, sir!"

"Take a look at Mike and tell me what you see."

"Yes, sir!"

When Jethro pulled aside the canvas covering the body, he recoiled with shock. "Jeezus! Mike's throat's been cut and he's turnin' black!"

The old man's jaw dropped, and he staggered. Jessie started to try and explain, but one of the Halverson men went for his gun; in that split second, she knew that the time for explaining and talking was over.

Ki's hand shot forward, and a *shuriken* flashed across the distance to bury itself in the face of the man who had reached for his six-gun. The blade caught the man just below his right eye. He screamed and then fell, twitching in his death throes.

Jessie's own hand went for her gun when she saw old Oliver Halverson go for the pistol hidden in his overalls. Fortunately, the weapon snagged on Halverson's pocket. Jessie heard the old man screech in rage even as she raised her six-gun, took a fraction of a second to steady her aim, and fired.

Halverson grunted like a pig and did a funny little hop-step when Jessie's bullet struck his massive chest. His gun tumbled to the ground. He stared at it as if he couldn't decide whether to reach for the fallen weapon or try and plug the leak in his chest.

Jessie shot him a second time; by now bullets were flying, and she turned her gun toward the other Halverson men who were shooting and dying. Even as she watched, one of the outlaw family took an arrow in the chest, and Ki pushed in front of Jessie and rudely knocked her over into the bed of the wagon so that she wasn't killed in the heat of the gun battle.

"Dammit!" Jessie cried as Scottie was blown out of his saddle by a rifle slug and two other riderless horses raced away.

She recoiled from Mike's body and came up firing until her gun was empty. Ki had leaped off the wagon seat and was attacking the Halverson men with a savagery that caused some to break and run. But there were still a good half dozen who were on their feet with guns blazing, and even as Jessie watched, another of her cowboys took a slug in the shoulder and tumbled from his horse.

Jessie had no idea who was winning or losing. She jumped from the wagon and snatched up a fallen cowboy's gun. Out of the corner of her eye, she saw Dustin intercept two of the fleeing Halverson men and gun them down.

Dustin shouted for her to drop, and when she didn't, he came racing toward her, his gun belching lead as enemies dropped in his path.

"Get down!" Dustin yelled, throwing himself into her so hard she was knocked flat.

Dustin covered her with his body and took a grazing bullet that was meant for Jessie. His hammer clicked on an empty, but Jessie raised and fired her gun at the onrushing wild man. Her slug tore into his gun and he slid forward on his knees right into both of them. Dustin whipped his pistol across the dying man's face and broke his nose. When he crashed forward, Dustin snatched the gun out of his hand and shot a ragged-looking man who was racing toward the ranch house. His bullet struck the man in the lower spine and he went down writhing, howling in agony.

Dustin took aim and put the man out of his misery with a marksman's shot to the back of his skull.

And then, just as soon as it had began, it was over. Jessie, dazed and shocked by the carnage, ran to Scottie, but he was dead. She jumped to her feet and moved from one fallen cowboy to the next. Three were dead, two wounded.

"What are we going to do now?" a cowboy asked as he frantically reloaded his six-gun. "What are we going to do now?"

Jessie's face was wet with tears. She sleeved them dry and said, "We unload Mike and get our dead and injured into this wagon and then we leave!"

Dustin, however, had other plans. He was already advancing on the ranch house; one of the survivors jumped outside and began firing wildly, but Dustin's slug knocked him back through the doorway.

An old, ugly woman in a shapeless dress rushed outside, screaming. She raised a big shotgun and pulled both triggers. Fortunately, she was so hysterical that her shot went far wide and she only killed one of the many barking yard dogs.

The woman dropped the shotgun, whirled, and raced back inside the cabin. Dustin kept marching toward the house, firing steadily.

"No!" Jessie shouted. "Ki, stop him!"

But it was too late even for the samurai, because Dustin was leaping onto the porch and ducking low and fast into the ranch house. Jessie heard the woman begin to scream, but her voice was drowned out by the roll of gunfire, six shots closely spaced.

Jessie's hand flew to her mouth and she started to run toward the house but Dustin emerged before she'd taken more than a few steps.

"You killed her?" Jessie gasped, not wanting to believe he could be so callous.

"Nope," he said, "but I did quiet her."

Jessie and Ki rushed into the house. The old harridan was on the floor, a nasty welt across her forehead. The last two Halverson men were sprawled close by, guns in their dead hands.

"Let's get out of here," Jessie said.

"Good idea," Dustin replied as they headed toward the wounded and the wagon.

Jessie was sick at heart about the loss of Scottie and her other cowboys. Fortunately, the wounded appeared as if they would recover. But it had been a terrible fight—and a costly one.

"I'm going to be leaving," Dustin said. "I've caused more than enough trouble for you."

Jessie knew it was true. Rarely had she felt so attracted to a man, but rarely had one caused so much death and destruction in so short a time.

"We can talk about it later," she said.

"Nothing to talk about. I'll help you get these men back to your ranch, then I'm gone."

"All right," Jessie replied, knowing that it was probably for the best.

★

Chapter 17

All eyes were on Dustin when he and Jessie returned to the Circle Star Ranch. They dismounted in grim silence. Jessie motioned Dustin to join her on the porch steps. She turned to address her men.

"What happened at the Halverson place was a tragedy," she began. "And I cannot possibly come up with any words that can adequately express my sorrow for the men we have lost and those of you who are wounded. I can only say that we went to that place in a gesture of goodwill. Had any of us lost a son or daughter, we'd have wanted their bodies returned for a family burial."

Jessie took a deep breath. "But everything that could have gone wrong did go wrong, and now we are without some very good men. We are almost too few to do the roundup, but we'll do the best that we can. If anyone wishes to quit, say so now. I'll understand."

She waited for a moment, and, when no one stepped

forward, forced a brittle grin. "We'll start the roundup day after tomorrow."

As she turned to go inside, Jessie raised her eyes and looked at Dustin a moment before she said, "We really do need all the help we can get."

"What about the mustangs that have to be broken? I thought that you needed all the horseflesh you could get from that rough bunch."

"We did, before we rode off to the Halverson place. Can you rope and brand a calf?"

"It's been a good long while," he admitted, "but after a few days, maybe I could get the hang of it again."

"Then stay and help us," Jessie pleaded. "We need you."

Dustin struggled for a moment, then nodded. "All right. I'll stay."

"Good!"

When Jessie went inside to tell Ed Wright about their disastrous trip to Overton, Ki took charge. "Let's carry the wounded into the bunkhouse. Someone needs to ride to town and get the doctor."

"I will," Dustin said, but his offer was ignored as all the other hands stepped forward or raised their hands.

"Ted, do you feel up to it?" Ki asked.

"I do!"

"Good," Ki said, "Tell the doctor to bring plenty of bandages and medicine."

"I will," Ted promised.

"Hey, kid," Dustin said, following him. "I'll help you saddle your horse."

"Don't need your help," Ted replied.

"I'll help you anyway," Dustin growled as he followed Ted across the yard and into the barn.

Dustin grabbed a halter and lead rope. There were four horses in the barn and he said, "Which one do you want?"

"I'll take that big bay horse in the last stall," Ted answered. "He's fast and needs the work."

As Dustin retrieved the horse, Ted said, "You want to tell me what happened at the Halverson place, or do I have to wait to hear about it tonight in the bunkhouse?"

"They went crazy," Dustin said. "One of them opened fire and there was no choice but to do the same."

"How many of them were there?"

"We were outnumbered. But they were short on good sense and poor shots."

"I suppose you and Ki each killed a bunch?"

Dustin frowned. "I never keep count. I don't know about the samurai, but I can tell you that Miss Starbuck was in the thick of it, just the same as the rest of us."

Dustin grabbed a saddle and blanket and threw them up on the bay's back. He glanced over at the kid and saw that Ted looked very troubled. "What's wrong?"

"What's wrong? Is that what you asked?"

"Yep."

"Scottie is dead! So are three other of our men, and most of the rest are wounded."

"It was a hard fight," Dustin said. "There was no help for it. Miss Starbuck was trying to do the right thing and it turned out wrong. Sometimes, things just happen that way."

Ted was quiet for a minute. Then he said, "You attract trouble like rotting meat attracts flies."

"That's a rough way to put it," Dustin muttered, "but I guess it's true enough."

"Are you leaving?"

"No," Dustin said. "I'm going to stay and help Miss Starbuck on her roundup and *then* I'm leaving."

"So you'll be here when I get back."

"That's right." Dustin tightened the cinch on the bay and made certain that the stirrups were the proper length. "Why are you asking me these questions?"

"I just wanted to make sure you'd be here when I get back, that's all."

"And if I wasn't?"

"I'd never learn how to break mustangs the right way, now, would I?" he said, a smile tugging at the corners of his mouth.

"No," Dustin said, "I guess you wouldn't."

Dustin watched as Ted rode out of the barn and then raced off toward town.

"Are you staying?"

Dustin turned around to see the samurai regarding him closely.

"I'll stay on for the roundup," Dustin said. "Miss Starbuck is so shorthanded now I feel obligated to stay."

"Don't feel obligated," Ki said. "We could do it just fine without you."

"Well," Dustin replied, "I'm sure that you could but I feel at least partially responsible for all that trouble we had over at the Halverson place."

"That's because you *are* responsible," Ki said with a definite chill in his voice.

Dustin hooked his thumbs into his cartridge belt. "Why is it you don't like me?"

Ki said, "I just want what's best for Jessie."

"And that isn't me."

"Exactly," Ki said, his voice taking on an edge. "You're bad news, and if you bring any more trouble to Jessie, you're going to answer to me."

Dustin studied on that for a moment or two. "I respect a man who tells me what is on his mind. But I have to admit that I don't have a whole lot of respect for a male whore."

Ki blinked and then moved so swiftly that Dustin was caught unprepared. The samurai's right foot delivered a blow that connected solidly with Dustin's jaw and almost broke it. Dustin staggered and tried to attack, but his looping right hand connected with nothing but empty space. The hard edge of the samurai's hand slammed down at the base of Dustin's neck.

Somehow, Dustin kept his feet, ducked another punch, and grabbed Ki around the waist and bulled him into a post. The samurai grunted with pain; Dustin butted him in the face with the top of his head, trying to break his nose. Ki wrapped a leg around behind Dustin and tripped him, sending them both sprawling to the earth.

They both came up fighting and slightly dazed. Dustin attacked the samurai, who was the quicker, ducked under his punch and delivered a vicious foot strike to Dustin's solar plexus that doubled him up. Ki followed with a second punch that drove Dustin to his knees. Before he could recover, Ki knocked him out with a squeeze to certain pressure points.

Ki climbed to his feet and looked down at his unconscious opponent. The man was tough and without fear. Had he been trained in the art of hand fighting, he would have been a worthy opponent. But as it was, Dustin was simply a very tough and skilled fistfighter.

133

"You *are* trouble," Ki said, touching the rapidly swelling bruise just under his eye. "Big trouble. And shorthanded or not, I'd feel a lot better if you weren't on this year's roundup."

★

Chapter 18

Jessie reined her tall palomino up short and pulled her bandanna down from her face. The dust was thick and churning, but she wasn't about to complain.

"How many cattle do you estimate we've got this year?" she asked a cowboy named Bob.

"I'd say about three thousand. Most of 'em was off that eastern range, but we found almost seven hundred in them thickets to the south."

"It's almost as if the cattle knew we were shorthanded and wanted to cooperate," Jessie said. "We've only been out here two weeks—I can't believe we've got this thing wrapped up."

"It's especially amazin' that we're doing it without Ed and Scottie," Bob said. "But the weather has been perfect and the new men turned out to be top-grade cowboys."

"Yes," Jessie agreed, "they have."

"That Dustin fella," Bob offered, "didn't seem like much of a hand the first couple of days, but he got the hang of it real good. Why, he's even a pretty danged good roper, Miss Starbuck."

Jessie agreed.

"We ought to be in Amarillo with this herd by tomorrow night," Bob said. "Hope they got enough holding pens near the stockyards and that you get top dollar."

"So do I," Jessie said, her eyes ranging out just in time to see a big brindle-colored longhorn break from the herd and make a desperate dash for freedom toward some almost impenetrable thickets.

One of the Amarillo cowboys was after it in a flash, spurring his horse and twirling his rope. But the longhorn was too quick this time, and it ducked into the thickets before the rope could be cast.

"I guess we'll just have to wait and get that one next spring." Jessie figured that the bull was lost because the brush was so high and dense that a horseman risked his life if he went after the fleeing animal.

"That Sandy ain't going to wait," Bob said. "Look at that damned fool!"

Bob was right. Sandy was a "damned fool" for going after the wild Texas longhorn.

"Look!" Bob exclaimed, "Dustin is going in after the both of them."

Dustin *was* going into the brush. He'd seen the cowboy vanish and known that the man had made a big mistake. It was impossible to rope a longhorn in that thick brush. A man following on horseback was just inviting disaster because if the longhorn came to a dead end, it would whirl, put its back to the wall, and charge the horseman. In the tight confines of those brushy tunnels, the longhorn would have every advantage and usually would succeed

136

in goring a cowboy's pony. Once it fell, the cowboy himself was often the longhorn's next victim.

"Hey!" Dustin yelled as he ducked his head and let his horse plunge into the brush and pick its way after the cowboy. "Come back out of there!"

But the cowboy wasn't coming, and Dustin wasn't about to turn around and quit this chase without a fight. His hat was knocked away by an overhanging piece of brush but he kept moving forward, amazed by the labyrinth of tunnels that kept opening on both sides.

About fifty yards into the brush, Dustin came to a huge open space, like a barn with no roof.

"Sandy!"

The cowboy appeared a moment later spurring his horse and Dustin saw why. The longhorn had turned and charged, driving Sandy into a full-fledged retreat. Sandy's horse stepped into a badger hole and did a complete somersault, hurling its rider into the brush. The longhorn charged the helpless cowpony. Before Dustin could drag his carbine from its scabbard, the fight was over and the horse was dying—the result of a horn driven deep into its exposed gut.

"Damn!" Dustin swore in anger as he frantically levered a shell into the carbine.

Sandy saw the longhorn lower its head and again bury its wicked horn into his pony's gut. He heard the horse trumpet in pain and saw it go down and slam its head against the earth. Sandy watched as the bull retracted its bloody horn from the horse and began to paw the earth. He twisted around and began to crab toward the wall of brush. It was so thick that he wasn't sure that he could even escape, but he was damn sure going to try.

Rifle shots echoed in the tight, brushy confines as

Dustin's Winchester boomed twice. The vicious bull collapsed and began to thrash in death. Dustin rode his horse over to Sandy's dying mount and mercifully shot it in the head. He jammed his rifle into its saddle boot, climbed down, and squatted on his heels.

"You all right, Sandy?"

"Yeah, I think so."

"How come you did something so foolish as to come in here after that longhorn?"

"I dunno," Sandy admitted. "I'd been hazin' that brindle for the last three days, and it kept breaking for freedom. Each time, either me or one of the others would rope it in time to stop the escape. I swore it wouldn't be different this time. I just had my mind fixed on that."

"Getting your mind fixed on one thing can be ruinous," Dustin said, grabbing Sandy's arm and hauling him to his feet. "You almost got yourself killed."

"I deserve to be horse-whipped for being so foolish," Sandy admitted. "I truly do."

"Well," Dustin said, "we'll leave that up to Miss Starbuck. As far as I'm concerned, the matter is finished. Let's yank your saddle and bridle and throw them over the back of my saddle and get the hell out of here."

"Suits me," Sandy said, looking both dazed and devastated. "Dustin?"

"Yeah?"

"Do you think that longhorn would have killed me like it did my poor horse?"

"I don't know," Dustin admitted. "You were scramblin' for cover. It depends on if you could have squeezed into the brush far enough or not. But it's so thick I'd say that a rattlesnake would have had

138

a hard time findin' a hole big enough to avoid gettin' tromped by that damned bull."

"Yeah," Sandy said, "I think I was a goner for sure. Thanks for saving my bacon."

"No problem," Dustin said.

When the two men finally emerged, Jessie was fit to be tied. She lit right into Sandy. "What were you thinking about when you went in there? It made about as much sense as climbing into a grizzly bear's den!"

"I know," Sandy admitted sheepishly. "And it cost the best horse in my string. I'll pay you back for him after I collect my wages in Amarillo, Miss Starbuck."

"Are you quitting?"

Sandy looked up at her. "You mean I ain't fired?"

"No," Jessie said, "you're not fired. But you will pay for that horse."

"Why . . . why, thank you very much," Sandy said, looking very relieved. "That's more'n fair of you. I swear I'll never do a fool thing like that again."

"I'll hold you to that promise," Jessie said. "Now, what happened to that longhorn bull?"

"I had to shoot him," Dustin said, not looking one bit sorry.

"Well," Jessie said after a moment, "that's sure in keeping with your character."

Dustin gave her a wink, then touched the brim of his hat in a salute and rode away.

"He saved my life," Sandy confessed. "That longhorn gored my horse and was coming after me when Dustin opened fire. You should have seen him! He hit that bull just twice and both shots were through the heart.

I never seen a man shoot that way before. Ain't he something!"

"He's something, all right," Jessie admitted before she motioned him to climb up behind her and ride double back to their chuckwagon.

"I figure that horse you lost was worth about twenty-five dollars," Jessie said as they rode along.

"Thirty," Sandy said, his eyes growing misty and his voice thickening with emotion. "He was a first-class cowpony and just four years old. Anybody would have given you thirty for that horse."

"All right," Jessie said, "thirty dollars."

★

Chapter 19

The rest of the cattle drive went without mishap, and Jessie was in a generous mood when her herd was safely delivered to a cattle buyer from St. Louis.

"I'll have a check cut for you first thing tomorrow morning," the heavyset buyer promised as he mopped his brow with a handkerchief. "And I hope that we can do business every spring. You've raised some fine cattle. That's why my company was willing to pay top dollar."

"Which was expected but also appreciated," Jessie said. "According to my calculations, your check ought to be for about ten thousand dollars. Is that right?"

"We need to do a final tally," the buyer, Mr. Duncan, explained as he wadded his handkerchief up and stuffed it into his back pocket. "And our tally is done at the railroad car. We pay the railroad on a per-head basis, and we pay you what they say they're hauling east to our packinghouse."

"That sounds fair, but we've already made our count. I won't settle for anything less."

Duncan frowned. "Well, I can assure you that we won't come up with anything less. And, with that assurance, may I have the pleasure of your company for dinner?"

Jessie thought Mr. Duncan wanted a lot more than dinner. Oh, he was nice enough, but his eyes were bold and hungry. Jessie did not appreciate his familiarity or his off-colored little innuendos.

"I'm afraid I'll have to decline, Mr. Duncan."

"Are you sure?" he asked, unable to hide his immense disappointment. "I was hoping that we could . . ."

"I will be celebrating with my crew and then we'll be leaving for Circle Star in the morning."

"What a pity!" Duncan exclaimed. "I had hoped that we would have some time to get better acquainted."

" 'Acquainted?' "

"Well," he backpeddled, "you know. We could talk cattle, but that does get a little monotonous."

"I'm sure you have better things to do here in Amarillo, and I really need to return to my ranch. My foreman had to miss this year's roundup because of an injury."

"What a shame," Duncan said without any real attempt to sound convincing.

Jessie extended her hand. "I'll meet you at the bank first thing tomorrow morning for that check."

"And I shall have it," Duncan vowed, looking quite dejected. "But I'm accustomed to celebrating such a big sale with the owner and—"

"Well," Jessie said, cutting the man's whining protest short, "sometimes we have to live with a little disappointment."

Before Duncan could form some sort of rejoinder, she

left for her hotel. She had booked the entire top floor of the Madison for her cowboys and knew they would be waiting to hear from her.

They were collected at the top of the stairs, sprawled on the settee and lounging about on the floor, dusty and grinning.

"Well, Miss Starbuck," Ernie Blake said, "did you skin that cattle buyer like you did the last one?"

"I did pretty well," Jessie said, trying to hide a grin.

"Was he as soft as he looked?"

"He was . . . well, he seemed to be a little distracted."

The cowboys laughed, they knew exactly why Duncan had been distracted, for they hadn't missed the fact that Jessie had purposefully left the top two buttons of her blouse unbuttoned and had worn her tightest pants.

"But I'm not getting paid until tomorrow morning, when the bank opens," Jessie said.

The expectant faces of the cowboys sagged with disappointment. They had been hoping for an immediate payday and a big night on the town.

"Tomorrow?" one asked, as if he could not believe such a bad piece of news. It was traditional that the cowboys never got paid until the outfit got paid.

"That's right," Jessie said. "By the time we finally made the tally and agreed the price, the bank was closed."

"No money until tomorrow," Dustin said, looking more amused than disappointed. "That's real tough."

"Well," Jessie said after a long pause, "I guess I could advance a small loan to you men against your wages."

"You could?" Hank Crowley asked, eyes widening

with new hope. "I mean, that'd be all right?"

"I suppose. How much would you men like to have . . . against tomorrow's pay?"

They went into a quick huddle, and Ernie was the first to stick his head up and say, "We could use about . . . about twenty dollars apiece."

"I guess I could do that," Jessie said, reaching into her pants and producing a wad of greenbacks. "But it would about bust me until tomorrow."

"Well, now," Dustin said, "it wouldn't be very gentlemanly of us to expect a lady like yourself to go bust, even for one evening, would it?"

The cowboys looked as if they thought that Jessie ought to be able to stand one night busted, but honor dictated that they shake their heads.

"Nope," they said in somber unison, except for Ted Cotton, who chose the more formal, "No ma'am."

"Well," Jessie said, looking from one man to the next, "you boys are certainly gentlemen. However, I don't think it would be right not to at least stand the bunch of you a couple of rounds in the nearest saloon."

The cowboys brightened and Jessie added, "Let's all head over to the Red Pony Saloon and wash the trail dust down."

Jessie stood back and let her cowboys charge down the staircase and across the lobby. Only Dustin remained behind and he was grinning. "I'll bet you buy those cowboys more than one round, eh, Miss Starbuck?"

"I'll tell the bartender to keep a tab and let them have all they want," Jessie said.

"And what if they want more than drink?"

"You mean women," Jessie said, reading his mind.

"That's right."

144

"Like I said," Jessie repeated, "they'll have a tab—up to a limit."

Dustin cocked his arm and escorted Jessie down the stairs. "I guess I won't need anything more than a couple of drinks tonight, wouldn't you agree Miss Starbuck?"

Jessie felt her cheeks warm because she knew what Dustin was driving at. After a few drinks, they would both wind up in her bed for the rest of the night.

Ten minutes later, the whiskey was flowing like water at the Red Pony and the Circle Star cowboys were laughing, hooting, and having one hell of a good time. Jessie stayed an hour, drinking with her cowboys and enjoying their company until the whiskey started getting the better of their good sense, and then she slipped on back to the hotel. About ten minutes later, there was a soft knock at her door as Dustin quietly arrived to make love to her.

It took them a few breathless moments to get into bed and get right down to business. Jessie wrapped her legs around Dustin's waist and had a wonderful time until they both lay exhausted and satisfied.

"What happens now?" she asked when they were both lying still within each other's arms.

"We have a long, pleasurable night," he promised.

"No," Jessie said, "I mean *tomorrow*."

Dustin sat up on the bed and studied her for a moment before he said, "Are you asking me if I'm going back to the Circle Star with you?"

"I guess I am."

"I can't," he said finally. "I've been doing a lot of thinking, and I can't put off going down to settle that old debt against my father and mother's killers."

"Maybe . . . maybe time has settled the debt for you,"

Jessie said. "Dustin, I wish that you would just . . ."

"Forget what happened back when I was a kid?" Dustin's voice shook with anger. "How they blew my father's face away with a shotgun and killed my mother? How they kept sending hired gunmen to find and kill me?"

When Jessie didn't answer, he lowered his voice and added, "Uh-uh, Miss Starbuck. I can't just forget about that and let bygones be bygones. I couldn't live with myself if I allowed those bloody bastards to get off scot-free."

"But you'll probably be killed."

"Better dead than to live feeling guilty and ashamed of myself. Besides," Dustin added, managing a smile, "I'm not afraid of dying. Sometimes, living can be a whole lot worse."

"But we could have something together . . . maybe," Jessie said, feeling a little foolish, but also desperate to talk him out of getting himself killed.

"Are you proposing to me?" he asked with a half-smile.

"I was just thinking that we could work out some better arrangement. Maybe I could help you buy a little cattle ranch."

He barked a laugh that was not pleasant. "Lordy, Miss Starbuck! Do you really think I'd be a kept man?"

"Of course not!" she snapped in anger. "You'd have to work your butt off in order to make a profit and stay in business, just like any other rancher."

"But you'd be there to bail me out if I got into hot water, wouldn't you?"

"I'd do what I could to help," Jessie said, her voice trailing off as she realized how she sounded. "I just don't want you to ride south and get killed."

Dustin enfolded Jessie in his arms and rocked her back and forth. Then he gently pushed her away and climbed out of the bed.

"What are you going to do?" she asked.

"I'm getting dressed, and then I'm getting the hell out of here while I can still muster up that much pride."

"Pride has nothing to do with it."

"Oh, yes, it does," he countered, pulling on his pants. "Someday, if I kill those men before they kill me, I'll come back and we can talk about a 'better arrangement.' But not now, Miss Starbuck."

"Jessie!" she cried. "Call me Jessie!"

"No," he said softly, "I feel better with Miss Starbuck. It reminds me of what different worlds we live in and how far above me you really are."

Jessie sprang out of bed, furious. "I'm not above you! For crying out loud, all I want to be tonight is *under* you! Is that so hard to understand?"

He took her back into his arms, and Jessie pressed her face to his shoulder, crying.

"I'll be back some day," he vowed. "And if I don't go now, you wouldn't want me to stay very long. I'd turn completely sour with self-hate. It's already starting to happen. I *have* to go, Jessie. You need to understand that revenge is like a sickness that won't stop spreading until it's cut clean away."

"By killing your enemies?"

"Yes," he said emphatically. "Because they deserve to be killed."

Jessie sighed. "I don't know that I'll be willing to take you back with so much blood on your hands."

"You can make up your mind then," he said, reaching

for his boots. "Either way, you do what you have to do."

"And to hell with everyone else?" she asked. "Is that your creed?"

Dustin reached for his gunbelt and slowly buckled it around his narrow waist. "Jessie, I'm not going to tell you good-bye because that means that I might not see you again. So, I'll just say so long for awhile."

And then, before Jessie could beg for him to change his mind, Dustin was gone.

★

Chapter 20

Dustin found it very difficult to walk away from Jessie and her Circle Star cowboys. He had surprised himself by the way he'd taken to working with that outfit and even enjoying a roundup again. That had made saying good-bye to Jessie far harder than expected.

Now, as he saddled Charlie and prepared to ride for the Rio Grande, he was filled with sadness, wondering if he'd survive to pass through this way again.

"Dustin?"

He turned to see young Ted Cotton standing by the barn door. Ted was holding a couple of bottles of beer but he didn't look a bit drunk. "Want one?"

"No, thanks," Dustin said. "How come you're not with the rest of the cowboys, celebrating?"

"I was, but I saw you crossin' the street with your saddlebags." Ted moved further into the barn, his eyes flicking from Dustin to his horse. "You goin' somewheres?"

"I suddenly got the itch to ride so I'm heading out,"

Dustin replied, not looking at the kid. "The herd is sold; there's no need for me to stay on any longer."

"Did Miss Starbuck fire you or something?"

"Nope. It's just time for me to go," Dustin said. "That's all."

"Well, you did just fine on the roundup and the trail drive. I'm sure that she'd like for you to stay on the payroll. Hell, Dustin, we all would! You saved Sandy's life in the thickets and we figured that—"

"Whatever you figured," Dustin said, cutting the kid short, "you figured wrong. The truth is, I've no intention of becoming a cowboy."

"Well, of course not!" Ted exclaimed. "You're a horse breaker and trainer. Everybody knows that."

"I got plenty of other things to do," Dustin said, reaching down to pick up and inspect one of Charlie's hooves.

"Like what?"

"Personal."

"You were going to show me how to work with horses," Ted blurted. "I was planning on being your helper and then maybe someday becoming a horse breaker and trainer myself."

"You can still do that," Dustin said, using his knife to clean the foot and then dropping it to the ground before straightening. "You have an easy, natural way with horses. They like you and you'll do fine if you remember what I've taught you so far."

"You haven't taught me *that* much yet," Ted dared to argue.

Dustin said nothing as he moved around his horse inspecting and cleaning out all of Charlie's hooves. The horse needed a new set of shoes, but that could wait a week—maybe even until he got to Laredo. Dustin tightened his cinch, thinking that he was pretty damned broke. He should have asked Jessie for his pay, but he was too proud. Besides, she'd given him a whole lot more than money could ever buy.

"You're going to wade into big trouble down along the Rio Grande, aren't you?"

Dustin slipped the halter off of Charlie and reached for his bridle. "Who told you that?"

"I just heard." Ted fidgeted for a moment, then said, "Everyone is saying that your father was Major Gideon Gamble."

There was a long silence as Dustin tied his saddlebags and bedroll behind the cantle. "Who came up with that story?"

"I dunno." Ted swallowed dryly. "They were tellin' the story about how the major was ambushed along the Rio Grande and his wife was . . ."

Ted's voice died and he stared at Dustin's face which had turned pale. "You *are* Major Gamble's son," he whispered. "I can tell it by the look on your face."

"Yes," Dustin said in a voice that did not sound as if it belonged to him.

"And he taught you how to use a gun and a rifle."

"Of course he did!" Dustin snapped. "My father understood better than anyone that only the strong will survive out here."

"Are you goin' to kill them—the ones that killed your mother and father? Is that what you're goin' to do next?"

Dustin was suddenly in a big hurry to leave Amarillo. Too much had been said between himself and this kid. A kid who was gazing at him with something akin to hero

151

worship, which made Dustin very uncomfortable.

"Good luck," was all he said as he mounted Charlie and rode out of the barn, turning south on a long trail that would take him straight down to Laredo.

"I want to come with you!" Ted shouted, running up alongside Charlie.

"Don't be crazy! You got a job breaking mustangs for Miss Starbuck."

"I can always come back to that. So could you, Dustin! But after we kill them fellas that gunned down your folks. After that, Dustin!"

"Go back to the saloon and get drunk and get laid with the other cowboys," Dustin growled, touching his spurs to Charlie's hide.

"I'm comin' along with you!" Ted shouted. "I'm drawin' our pay in the morning and then I'm catchin' up with you!"

"No!" Dustin shouted as he galloped out of town heading south.

Ted Cotton guzzled down both beers and hiccupped, then turned and walked across the street toward the saloon. He went inside, but he didn't feel like joining in the fun.

"Ted?"

He turned to face Ki, who was watching him closely. "Yeah?"

"Come here," Ki ordered.

They moved off to a quieter corner of the saloon where Ki took a chair with his back to the wall. Ki said, "You went to see Dustin ride out." It wasn't a question.

"Yeah, and it's all true. He is Major Gamble's son. The one that they tell about vanishing before he could be murdered like his parents."

"I see." Ki steepled his fingers. "Did Dustin say where he was going?"

"To Laredo."

"I guess that's what he has to do."

"I'm going after him," Ted said, chin raising in slightly drunken defiance. "I'm going to have to quit the outfit and ride south to Laredo."

"Why?"

The question was natural enough but it seemed to catch the kid off guard. "Why?"

"If Dustin Gamble has a fight, then it's *his* fight, not yours."

Ted chewed on that for a moment, then shrugged. "Cowboys ought to stick together, Ki. You know that."

"I know that Dustin isn't a cowboy and never will be. Not in the heart."

Ted suspected that this was true but his mind was made up. "Well, I'm going after him anyway. After we kill all them folks down in Laredo, we'll come back and see if Jessie will give us back our jobs."

Ki could see that there was little use in arguing with the stubborn kid. Ted was determined to go after Dustin, but that might change in the morning after he was sober and could see things more clearly.

Ki went to bed, his own mind in no small amount of turmoil. On the one hand, he thought it was all for the best that Dustin had chosen to ride south, probably to his death. The man was a killer and bad news. On the other hand, Ki admired Dustin's grit and determination. According to the legends about the famed Confederate Army officer, the man had been cold-blooded but had also possessed a rigid code of honor. A code of honor that Dustin also held inviolate because he had never

153

ambushed or back-shot his enemies. To the contrary, Dustin had killed every one of them in fair fights after calling them out and issuing each one ample warning to defend themselves.

Maybe, Ki thought, the men that Dustin intended to shoot really did deserve to die. One thing could not be denied, and that was that Dustin was a warrior. A worthy opponent and a man who felt honor-bound to bring a swift and final justice to his sworn enemies.

Ki could understand and even admire that. Still, Dustin Gamble was gone and, to the samurai's way of thinking, that was the best thing for everyone—especially Jessie.

★

Chapter 21

Jessie was paid for her herd of beef as promised the next morning. It was after ten o'clock when she finally managed to extract herself from the St. Louis cattle buyer and return to her hotel. The Circle Star cowboys were waiting for her, all bloodshot eyes and rueful grins.

"Looks like you boys had yourselves quite a night," Jessie said. "All right, who wants their pay now?"

Every man did. "Some of us," Bob confessed, "already spent it all."

Jessie wasn't surprised. Her men were smart and tough when it came to their work on horseback, but they had no concept of saving money. Some of them had been with her for a good many years and hadn't managed to accumulate anything of greater value than the clothes they wore, their spurs, saddles, and a good pair of boots.

Ted Cotton stayed in the background until all the others were paid, minus the previous day's advances.

Then he stepped forward, lowered his voice, and said, "Miss Starbuck, I'm going to Laredo to see if I can help Dustin."

Jessie blinked with surprise. "Why, Ted, you're no gunman."

"I know," the kid admitted, "but I can generally hit what I aim for with a rifle. I shot many a rabbit for my family before I started to cowboying."

"It's not the same. Dustin is going after the men who killed his parents. Even as good as he is, I have the feeling that he won't survive."

"Then how come you let him go?"

Jessie frowned. "Dustin does what he wants and won't take advice or orders. His mind was fixed on revenge."

"Well, you got a ranch to run, but I'm just a cowboy and I mean to help Dustin."

"You don't even have a rifle."

"Maybe not," Ted stuttered, "but . . . but I can use my pay to buy me a used one. Besides, I thought that you might want to give me Dustin's pay so's I could take it on down to him. I mean, if you trust me."

"Of course I trust you." Jessie said. "But I'm upset that you're determined to join Dustin. No good will come of this, Ted."

Ted took a deep breath. "I'm sorry, Miss Starbuck. I owe you plenty for takin' in a green kid when nobody else would give me a job. But going after Dustin is just something that I have to do."

Jessie could see that there was nothing to do but to pay the kid his and Dustin's wages.

"All right," she said, counting out their money. "And if you do catch up with Dustin, tell him we want him back no matter what happens in Laredo."

"I'll do 'er," Ted promised. "For sure I'll tell him, Miss Starbuck."

"I'll let you have my extra Winchester. At least then I'll know that you have something that will shoot straight and not jam or misfire in a crisis."

"You're sure generous, Miss Starbuck."

"Wait here," Jessie ordered, heading for her room to get the rifle.

But somewhere about in the middle of the stairs, Jessie knew that she couldn't just allow the idealistic kid to go racing off by himself to Laredo, probably to get killed along with Dustin.

"Dammit," Jessie swore as she grabbed up her saddlebags, rifle, and other belongings. "I'm going with him."

Before she could get out of the hotel, all the Circle Star cowboys were in a heat to follow Dustin down to Laredo. Jessie had to raise her arms for silence.

"Now, listen," she said, "Ed Wright is alone back at Circle Star and there's a big ranch that still needs to be run. So you're all going back except for Ted and me."

"I'm coming, too," Ki said gravely.

"Of course," Jessie said, correcting herself. "Although I know the low opinion you have of Dustin."

"I am here to protect you," Ki said. "Dustin has very little to do with that."

"I understand." Jessie turned to Ted. "When did Dustin leave town last night?"

"About ten o'clock. I tried to talk him out of it but he wouldn't listen. He may be a killer," Ted added, "but he's got a lot of good in him. That's why I have to go and try to help save his hide."

"Me, too," Jessie confessed. "Me, too."

157

She looked over at the samurai but could not catch his eye. One thing Jessie did know for certain was that Ki was not pleased. But he would go and he would fight.

"Dustin doesn't realize it yet," Jessie said, "but help is on the way."

"I just hope that we can catch Dustin before he gets to Laredo," Ted said in a worried voice. "He's the kind of man that can get a lot out of a horse."

"So can we," Jessie promised as she headed swiftly toward the livery.

Fifteen minutes later they were galloping out of Amarillo with Jessie in the lead on her handsome palomino, Sun. Jessie was tired, for she had not slept well, tossing and turning all the previous night worrying about Dustin.

"Do you think we have any chance of catching him before he arrives in Laredo?" Ted asked when they stopped at noon beside a quiet stream to rest and allow the horses to graze.

"I don't know," Jessie confessed. "It depends on how hard he's pushing to get there. It must be over five hundred miles to Laredo. Anything can happen when you have to go that kind of distance."

"You think we can make it in a week?" Ki asked.

"Barring any catastrophes, yes." Jessie came to her feet, anxious to leave. "But a lot depends on the weather, if we come across Indians, and if our horses hold up to the pace."

"We've better horseflesh under us than Dustin," Ted told them. "That Charlie is game, but he's getting up in years."

"He's tough, though," Jessie said. "Just like the man who rides him."

Ki supposed that was true enough, but there was no doubt in his mind whatsoever that they would overtake Dustin before another full day had passed. The question then was, would Dustin raise hell and even allow them to accompany him to Laredo?

Maybe Jessie hadn't considered that a possibility, but Ki had, and it was of no small concern.

On the second day out of Amarillo, they spotted a man walking his horse. Jessie exclaimed. "That's got to be him!"

"His horse must have gone lame," Ki said.

"He's going to be steamin'," Ted added. "Dustin thinks one hell of a lot of that old horse."

"Well," Jessie said, pushing Sun into a gallop, "let's catch up with him and find out what happened."

When Dustin realized that he was being followed, he drew his rifle and sat down to wait. When he recognized Jessie, Ki, and Ted, he jammed his rifle back into its boot and thumbed back his hat brim.

"What are you three doing here?"

"Ted reminded me that you forgot your pay."

"And you rode all the way down here to deliver it?" Dustin asked with a very skeptical look on his handsome face.

"We thought we ought to ride down and see what Laredo has to offer these days," Jessie said, dismounting and extending Dustin his pay. "Hope you don't mind."

"I *do* mind," Dustin said, barely able to curb his anger. "You'll only get shot in Laredo."

"Nothing in life is guaranteed," Ki said, "unless it's the loyalty of friends."

"You're not a friend," Dustin told the samurai. "You're

159

just tagging along because of Jessie."

Jessie's green eyes flashed with anger. "Ki is here because he understands that some wrongs must be righted. Ted was willing to follow you by himself."

"Well," Dustin groused, "all three of you are riding into more trouble than you realize. There's a rattlesnake den in Laredo that has to be cleaned out, and someone is bound to be poisoned before it's finished."

Jessie avoided Dustin's challenging gaze. She walked over to Charlie and rubbed the horse's shoulder. "What happened to your horse?"

"Rock bruise," Dustin said with a sad shake of his head. "I should have had new shoes put on him, but I was in a hurry to leave."

"I noticed," Jessie said, picking up Charlie's right front foot and examining it carefully. "It's not so bad."

"Bad enough to lame him up for a couple of weeks."

"Maybe it's a sign that you shouldn't go on to Laredo."

Dustin snorted. "And maybe it's a sign that I shouldn't have ridden him over that dry riverbed with all those sharp rocks yesterday."

Jessie was starting to get irritated with Dustin. "Listen," she said, "do you want to ride double, or would you rather walk to Laredo by yourself?"

"I'm not sure," Dustin said after a minute. "But . . . aw, I'll ride double as long as it's behind you."

Jessie caught the look in his eyes; no doubt Ted and Ki did as well. She climbed up on Sun. "Come on, we've got a long ride ahead of us."

"I might have to buy another horse and leave Charlie somewheres until that rock bruise heals," Dustin said, looking pretty dejected.

"There's a town called Prideful about twenty miles to the south of us," Jessie said. "I guess we could find you another horse there and strike out early tomorrow morning."

Dustin patted his jeans. "Well, thanks to you, at least I have enough money to board Charlie while he recovers as well as buy me a replacement."

"Not much of one, though." Jessie knew that Dustin only had forty dollars.

"I'll worry about that when the time comes," Dustin said, slipping his arm tightly around Jessie's waist before placing his hand on her upper thigh.

"Watch those hands," Jessie warned under her breath.

Dustin chuckled and squeezed her tight. "I'm glad you three decided to come along," he confessed. "I was thinking that it was going to be one hell of a long trip back down to the Rio Grande."

Jessie smiled, liking the feel of Dustin's body pressing up tight against her back. Maybe, she thought, if Sun was up to it, they could ride double an extra day or two.

★

Chapter 22

"It hasn't grown much since I was here five years ago," Jessie said as she wearily climbed down from her horse and let her men call for the liveryman to take their exhausted, dusty horses.

"Laredo is a tough town," Dustin said, his eyes haunted by the memories of his childhood. "My father owned a big mansion at the end of town and a small ranch down along the Rio Grande. We used to swim in that river during the hot summer days and then cross it at night to steal Mexican horses and cattle."

"Didn't you ever get caught?"

"Sure."

"And wasn't that pretty dangerous?"

"Men took risks on both sides of the border. I knew what could happen, even when I was very young."

"I can't imagine a father taking his son on such a dangerous foray. Especially when it wasn't necessary."

"How do you know it wasn't necessary?"

"It's common knowledge that the major was a wealthy man."

Dustin laughed without humor. "My father was a drinker and a gambler. He was brave and dashing and I loved him, but he squandered every dime he made in saloons, gambling halls, and Mexican cantinas. He died owing far more than he was worth and his many creditors were bitter because of the debts they could never collect."

"I see," Jessie said. "Dustin, it's small wonder that your life hasn't been exactly trouble free."

"My life has had its share of troubles, all right," Dustin admitted as he dismounted from the sorrel gelding they'd bought to replace Charlie while he recuperated. "But I tell you something, if it all ends tonight, I can at least say I've loved and been loved by Jessica Starbuck, the most beautiful woman in Texas."

"Shh!" Jessie scolded, feeling herself blush with pride.

"Aw, hell," Dustin said. "Both Ki and the kid know why we went sneaking off together every night. They're not blind."

"I know," Jessie said, "but I still cling to a shred of propriety."

"You'll get over it," Dustin assured her.

"How long you three stayin'?" the liveryman asked.

"We don't know," Dustin told him. "Could be a few hours, or it could be a few days."

The liveryman, an old and bent man called Hoop, led their horses inside and began to unsaddle them, his mouth working hard on a chew of tobacco. Jessie could see that Hoop was good at his job: his stalls were clean and the horses in his care well-fed and well-groomed.

"Cost you two dollars a day for the four horses," Hoop called over his shoulder. "Five days' board due in advance."

"We won't be here that long," Dustin said with grim certainty.

"Maybe you will and maybe you won't. I'll refund unless you want these animals grained extra and their shoes replaced. They're pretty thin and I'm still about the best in the business."

"You don't look well enough to diaper a baby," Dustin said with a wink.

The liveryman glanced back, spat tobacco, and then chuckled. "I reckon I'm well enough to shoe these horses, sonny. So what brings you four to Laredo?"

Dustin's expression grew somber. "Hoop, I've come to pay a visit to some old friends. Maybe you could tell me where they can be found."

"Maybe," the liveryman said, not looking at Dustin as he removed Sun's bridle and closed the stall door behind the palomino. "Miss, do you want him curried and cleaned up? Too pretty a horse to look so rough."

"Sure," Jessie said, her attention fixed on Dustin.

"I asked you a question, oldtimer," Dustin said, moving over to the liveryman. "I need to locate four men and I'd sort of like to surprise them. Bob Kilrain, Jack Trump, Henry Gunter, and Alonzo Cobb."

"All mighty important citizens," Hoop said, finally looking right at Dustin. "Pillars of the community, you might say."

"I never expected them to live long enough to gain respectability," Dustin said. "Ten years ago, they were thieves and murderers."

"Time changes a lot of things," Hoop said, spitting.

164

"And some things never change," Dustin said, his voice low and hard.

"Who *are* you?" Hoop asked. "You don't tell me, I don't tell you anything. That's the way it's going to work."

Dustin seemed to make up his mind. He glanced sideways at Jessie, Ki, and Ted, then turned back to the liveryman. "Did you ever have the honor of knowing Major Gideon Rutherford Gamble?"

Hoop stopped chewing and spitting. "You're his kid, ain't you? The one that they tried to kill."

"That's right," Dustin said in a brittle voice.

"And you come to pay back them that killed your mother and your father."

"You're smarter than you look, oldtimer."

"And these three are going to help you?"

"No," Dustin emphatically stated. "They're not a part of this. They're just . . . just along for the show."

"Then they'll see you either shot or hanged," Hoop predicted. "Because the men you're after have the law on a leash. Even if you did get lucky enough to kill them, you'd be arrested and hanged."

"Where are they?"

Hoop frowned, chewed, and said, "Let's see. Bob Kilrain owns a freighting business at the north end of town. He also runs a stageline and buys and sells horses back and forth across the border, most of which are stolen."

"What about Jack Trump?"

"He's the banker. Richest man in town."

"Where does he live?"

"Got a mansion about three blocks west of us. Big red and white thing. You can't miss it."

165

"Does he live alone?"

"Got a wife, but she's almost as sickly as he is. They have a maid and a houseman, both of 'em are good folks and—"

"I won't hurt them. Anyone else?"

"He's got a man named Duke that sticks pretty close to him. Duke has a gunman's reputation, although Trump would argue that fact."

"And Henry Gunter?"

"He died about three months ago. Choked on a piece of meat over at the Plaza House Restaurant."

"I hope he died slow," Dustin said.

"He did."

"Good. What about the last one, Alonzo Cobb?"

"Mr. Cobb has a big ranch about three miles north of us. He's done just fine. Like Kilrain, he deals with stolen livestock and seems to make out pretty well. He's got a couple of sons, mean bastards. He'll be the toughest to drop."

Dustin seemed satisfied. "All right," he said, turning to his friends. "You heard what Hoop said. If you become a part of this, you're liable to get hanged. So, it's my show, is that understood?"

Jessie took a deep breath and expelled it slowly. "All right. It's your show."

"Then it's settled," Dustin said, pulling out his six-gun and making sure that it was ready for action. "I'll start with Kilrain, then Trump, then Alonzo Cobb. Cobb's the one that deserves to die the hardest, and I want to take my time."

Jessie opened her mouth to protest but something in Dustin's eyes told her that she would only be wasting her breath.

★

Chapter 23

Dustin turned to Ki and said, "I don't want any of you to be a part of this. Why don't you take the lady to a hotel and relax."

Ki looked to Jessie and Ted. "Why don't we take his advice?"

"All right," she heard herself say. She turned to Dustin. "On one condition."

"Let's hear it," he said, dropping his Colt into its holster and then reaching for his rifle.

"You don't kill anyone without giving them a fair chance. Otherwise, what's the point? You'll be just as guilty as they were for killing your mother and father."

"I disagree," he said in a low, hard voice. "They ambushed my father and executed a helpless woman. That's a thousand times worse than what I have planned for them."

Before Jessie could frame an argument, Dustin was moving out the barn door, heading up the street toward Bob Kilrain's freighting office. When he arrived, Dustin realized with no small degree of shock that he might not even recognize the three men that he had come to kill. It had been many years since he'd fled Laredo with hired killers hot on his heels. All that Dustin could remember about Kilrain was that he was a very big, loud, and profane man who was reported to be a dangerous knife fighter.

Dustin squared his shoulders and leaned his Winchester up against the front of the freighting office before he stepped inside. A man about his own age was sitting at a battered desk, furiously doing figures on a yellow pad of paper. When the man did not bother to even acknowledge Dustin's presence, Dustin reached down and clamped ahold of his wrist.

"You've poor manners. I might be an important customer."

The young man tried to pull free. He looked up angrily. "I saw you coming up the street; you don't look like a customer. I judge you for a horse trader and we're not buying."

Dustin backhanded the clerk so hard that the man crashed over in his chair. Before the clerk could recover, Dustin had a fistful of his shirt and was dragging him erect.

"Where is Kilrain?"

The man's eyes widened with fear. "Out . . . out back! But he's dickering with Señor Sanchez for some horses and—"

Dustin didn't wait to hear anymore. His fist crashed into the young man's jaw, knocking him out cold. Dustin dragged the unconscious clerk into what he supposed was Bob Kilrain's private office. The office looked prosperous, and that made Dustin all the more bitter.

Bob Kilrain was indeed dickering for horses, at least twenty of them, with six Mexicans who looked very rough. When they saw the look on Dustin's face, they stiffened and eased their hands toward their weapons. Kilrain, however, was too embroiled in his negotiations to even notice the intruder until Dustin pushed between him and Sanchez.

"What the hell!" Kilrain roared. "Gawdamn you, can't you see I'm busy here?"

"Not anymore, you aren't."

Kilrain blinked as confusion momentarily replaced anger and outrage. "Who the hell . . ."

Dustin's voice dropped to a whisper. "My name is Dustin Gamble and I'm your worst nightmare come to life."

Kilrain was wearing a gun but apparently figured a Bowie was the surer weapon at such close quarters. He was a veteran knife fighter and he stomped the heel of his boot down hard on Dustin's foot, trying to break bones as he drew his Bowie and drove it upward toward Dustin's exposed belly.

Gideon had taught Dustin well, but even so he was barely able to throw himself to one side before Kilrain's blade cut through his jacket.

Dustin recovered and smiled, drawing his own knife and holding it up before him. "How many men have you *really* fought? And I'm not counting the ones that you got from behind."

Kilrain's lips pulled back from his teeth. "I put a bullet in your pa and I'll send you to join him in hell!"

"We'll see," Dustin said, circling to his right, feinting again and again to test the older man's reactions. Kilrain was fifty pounds overweight and slow. Confident, Dustin pretended to stumble. When Kilrain foolishly went for the ploy, Dustin sliced him under the left arm, cutting to the bone so deep that he almost dismembered the freighter. Kilrain screamed and dropped his knife. Blood poured down his side.

"Pick it up," Dustin ordered, stepping back.

"No!" Kilrain was turning pale and shaking. "Sanchez!" he cried. "Shoot this man!"

Sanchez went for his gun but Dustin beat him to the draw and said, "Ride, amigo, and take your friends with you before I put a bullet through your fat head."

Sanchez suddenly decided that riding would be the smart thing to do. He whirled, shouted to his *vaqueros*, and then mounted his own horse. In a moment, they were gone, leaving only Kilrain and Dustin in the lot with a pen of stolen horses.

"Pick up the knife."

Kilrain shook his head.

"Then go for your gun, or I'll carve you up like a holiday turkey," Dustin warned.

Kilrain was losing blood fast and starting to shake. He looked deep into Dustin's eyes and a plea formed on his lips, but when Dustin took an advancing step, the freighter knew that there would be no mercy. He made a play for his Colt and Dustin hurled the Bowie. It spun three times and buried itself to the hilt in Kilrain's broad chest.

Dustin went over and studied the dead man, wondering why he didn't feel better.

"I let you die too damned easily," he said as he turned and walked up the street, toward Jack Trump's bank.

• • •

"I'm sorry," the teller behind the barred window said. "But Mr. Trump isn't in today. He's a bit under the weather. I'm sure that Mr. Jackson, our assistant manager, could help you."

"I don't think so," Dustin said easily.

"Can I tell him who called?"

"No," Dustin said pleasantly, "I'll tell him myself."

"He'll be in by ten o'clock, if he's feeling better."

"He won't be," Dustin predicted confidently.

"Huh?"

Dustin didn't bother to explain. There was no more time to be wasted. Dustin wanted to kill the banker before the alarm was sounded and be on his way out to settle with Alonzo Cobb, the man reported to have blown Gideon Gamble's head to pieces with a shotgun.

The mansion was impressive for a tough bordertown like Laredo. Two stories high, it was freshly painted, and had a rose garden and a manicured lawn. When Dustin knocked at the door, a maid answered.

"Yes, sir?"

"I'm sorry to bother, but I'd like to see Mr. Trump."

"I'm afraid he's not feeling well," the older woman said. "Perhaps you could come back some other time, or—"

"I'll see him right now," Dustin said, shoving the door open and moving inside.

"Sir!" the maid cried, her frightened gaze jumping to the ornate wooden staircase that led to the upstairs bedrooms. "You can't go up there."

"Sure I can," Dustin said, taking the stairs two at a time. At the top of the landing, he looked down a hallway with two doors on each side. He tried the first

171

one and saw a frail woman reading a book. When their eyes met, she dropped her book and seemed about to cry out with alarm until Dustin smiled disarmingly and said, "Sorry to have disturbed you, Mrs. Trump."

Dustin closed the door, hearing the woman call for the maid. He tried the second and when it opened he saw a man of about thirty years of age reading a dime novel of the Old West. He was reclining on his bed with his shoes off and there was a gunbelt hanging from his bedpost. This, Dustin knew, would be the hired gunman named Duke.

"Who the hell are you?"

"You don't want to know. Just keep reading."

Duke was still staring when Dustin slammed his door and moved up the hall to the last door.

"Hello, there," Dustin said after entering to find the banker sitting at a desk wearing silk pajamas. "Taking the day off, are we?"

"Who the hell are you?"

"Dustin Gamble. You know me, Mr. Trump. You've spent a lot of money over the years trying to avoid this meeting. Too bad it was all wasted."

Trump was withered and his face was pinched, indicating poor health. His eyes, blue orbs sunk deep in the sockets of his bony face, reflected great physical suffering.

"So," he said, coming to his feet and pulling his satin dressing robe around his thin frame, "you've come back to haunt me like a ghost from the past."

"I guess I have," Dustin said, "only I'm not a ghost."

"You're going to kill me?" Trump took a deep, shuddering breath. "Go ahead. I'm already dying, so draw your gun and end my misery. At least I'll go to hell knowing you'll soon follow."

The man's calm fatalism defused Dustin's quiet rage. "What are you dying of?"

"A tumor."

Dustin realized that the man was telling the truth. He walked over and picked up a bottle of medicine. "What is this?"

"Laudanum. But it barely cuts the pain."

"How much time has the doctor given you?"

"Six more months, but you're going to spare me that agony."

The smell of medicine and sickness made Dustin's stomach churn. He didn't remember what Trump had looked like before, but he would never forget what the tortured, pain-wracked man looked like now.

"Have a nice, long death," Dustin said, holstering his gun and heading for the door.

He heard a strangled cry and whirled to see Trump with a derringer in his fist. The banker fired but he was in such poor health that the shot was ridiculously wild.

"Maybe you ought to reload and kill yourself, if you've the guts," Dustin said.

Trump cursed, but Dustin just slammed the door. He was halfway down the stairs when Duke jumped out of his room with a gun in his fist.

"Hey!" Duke shouted.

Dustin spun and dropped to one knee as his gun came up solid in his fist. Both fired at almost the same instant and both hit their targets. Dustin felt as if someone had punched him in the shoulder, slamming him over to tumble down the stairwell.

Duke beat him to the ground floor, pitching through

173

the upper-floor railing and landing face-down on the gorgeous Italian marble floor near the dining table.

"Sorry for the mess," Dustin said through clenched teeth as he passed the gaping maid and hurried outside.

★

Chapter 24

"You can't go out to that man's ranch in this shape!" Jessie said as she examined the bullet wound in Dustin's shoulder. "We need a doctor to take this slug out and then you need—"

"I need to finish this," Dustin gritted through clenched teeth. "More than anything in the world, I need to finish what I came to Laredo for."

"Even if you bleed to death doing it?"

"Yes," he hissed. "At least then I'd die knowing that I'd tried to avenge the murder of my mother and father."

Jessie looked at the samurai. "Go hire a buggy from Hoop. Bring it around the back of the hotel. We'll meet you there in fifteen minutes."

"What about Ted?"

Jessie had already given that a good deal of thought. Ted Cotton worshipped Dustin and he was just young and foolish enough to get them all killed. "Put him to sleep for a good long while."

"I agree," Dustin said. After Ki left, he added, "Jessie, after this is over, just collect Ted and hurry on back to your ranch."

Jessie pursed her lips tightly together and tore the bed sheets into bandages. "So tell me. If by some miracle, you survive this, what happens then?"

"What do you mean?"

"You'll become a wanted man."

"Why? Both Kilrain and Duke tried to kill me first."

"Any witnesses?"

Dustin shook his head. "When I killed Kilrain, we were alone. The Mexicans he'd been trading with rode off. And when I shot Duke, it was just the two of us, but he shot first."

"And you left the banker to die of his tumor."

"Seemed a more fitting end to the son of a bitch than a quick and merciful bullet."

"Even if I get you a good lawyer, you'll be found guilty and sent to prison, if not hanged."

"Then I've got nothing to lose by riding out to Alonzo Cobb's spread and finishing this business."

"No," Jessie said, feeling her throat tighten, "it would seem to me like you're damned if you do, and damned if you don't."

"Finish up that bandaging," Dustin ordered in a quiet voice. "I need to get moving. I'm starting to feel woozy. Maybe fresh air will bring me back."

Jessie helped Dustin to his feet a few minutes later.

"I want to be wearing my shirt and coat," he said. "When Alonzo first sees me, it's important that he doesn't have a clue that I'm hurt."

"All right," Jessie said. "But your shirt is bloodstained."

"I'll button up the coat."

"That's bloodstained too."

"But dark enough that he might not notice," Dustin argued.

Jessie bound the wound as tightly as possible, but she knew that it was still going to leak blood. "How far is the Cobb Ranch?"

"Hoop said just three miles. I could walk there if I had to. Jessie?"

She looked up into his eyes. "Yes?"

"Thank you for everything. I'm sorry it didn't work for us."

"That's all right," she said. "I knew from the very start that it wouldn't."

Even over the pain of his wound, Jessie saw that her words cut him deeply. Dustin tried to say something, then gave it up and shuffled to the door. He looked weak and unsteady; she took his arm and helped him down the hallway and out the back door to the wagon.

"Thanks to the both of you," Dustin said as they helped him up onto the seat.

Ki looked at Jessie and said, "Ted will have a nice, long sleep."

"Thanks," she said, glad that she didn't also have to worry about the kid in addition to everyone else.

Alonzo Cobb's AC Ranch looked downright humble by comparison to Jessie's huge Circle Star, but her experienced eye told her that this Rio Grande rancher ran a very profitable operation. The cattle that Jessie saw were in good condition and the range wasn't overgrazed like so many ranches down in this part of the country.

"There's the ranch house," Ki said. He looked to

177

Jessie, his eyes asking her what they were going to do.

"I don't know yet," she said. "We're going to let things unfold as they will. All I want to do is to make sure that Dustin has a chance."

The samurai nodded. Dustin forced a thin-lipped smile. "I sure wish you'd both just let me do this alone."

"Can't," Jessie heard herself say. "Just like you can't turn away even though you're bringing on your own destruction."

When they pulled into the ranch yard, two dogs came flying out from under the porch. They were collies of some type, big, multicolored, with long, sharp snouts.

"Look," Ki said, pointing up to the front door of the house. An older man and his two tall sons emerged from the house. They weren't smiling but at least they called off the dogs.

Alonzo Cobb was tall and stooped by the years but his face was still ruggedly handsome. He wasn't wearing a sidearm but his sons both packed six-guns. They came over to stand beside the wagon Jessie had rented.

Alonzo studied them a moment, his eyes lingering on Jessie but settling on Dustin and the spreading bloodstain soaking darkly through his coat.

He said, "Who are you and what do you want?"

Dustin took in a deep breath and said, "You're Alonzo Cobb."

"That's right," the older man snapped, "and who the hell are you and why are you sitting there bleeding?"

"I just killed Bob Kilrain in a knife fight," Dustin said after a moment. "But I let Jack Trump suffer from his sickness."

The rancher's eyes narrowed to slits. "And what does that have to do with me?"

"Everything and nothing," Dustin said, climbing down from the wagon and unbuttoning his coat. "Because you're the last man."

"The last man?"

"That I'm going to kill."

Alonzo stiffened and his sons moved a little closer, hands brushing the butts of their six-guns. "Easy, boys," the old man said. "Let's hear the man out before we decide what to do with him."

"The decision," Dustin grunted, "is *mine*."

Alonzo's eyes flicked up to Jessie and the samurai. He said, "You better tell this crazy, bleedin' bastard to raise his hands slow and easy and then get back into your wagon before you all get shot."

"Talk to *me*," Dustin hissed even as his hand swept down to his six-gun and it jumped up and lined on the rancher's chest. "Because I'm a Texas tornado that's about to blow away your miserable life."

"What's your damned name!" the rancher demanded.

"Dustin Gamble. Son of Gideon Gamble, the man whose head you blew off more than ten years ago."

Alonzo Cobb paled. His sons seemed to deflate as Dustin's gun barrel waved like a dark finger of death over them.

"I've got other men here. If you shoot me, all three of you will be gunned down. Is that what you want, Gamble? For the lady to die, too?" Cobb managed to blurt.

"No," Dustin said. "This is just between the two of us. Tell your sons to drop their guns and step back or I'll kill them, and then kill you."

"Do what he says," Cobb ordered.

The sons did as they were told.

"Now," Dustin said, dropping his own gun at his feet. "Things are even. Just you and me. Anytime you want to go for that gun, make the move."

Cobb grinned. "You're a fool, just like your father."

"Yeah," Dustin said, "I know. Now, go for it."

Cobb was old but he was smart. His hand whipped into his jacket and a hide-out gun materialized. He grinned, took aim, and would have killed Dustin if Ki's whirling *shuriken* star blade hadn't struck him in the throat and sent him backpeddling.

The two sons dove for their weapons but Dustin was already on his knees, sweeping up his six-gun.

"Don't," he whispered, his soft tone of voice terribly ominous. "Don't make me kill you, too."

The sons froze. The taller of the two said, "We'll find and kill you someday. All three of you."

Dustin's eyebrows raised. "Is that a promise?"

"It is," the man said, his face white with rage.

"He's right," the shorter brother vowed. "We'll kill all three of you."

"I believe you," Dustin said, his voice suddenly old. "You've got your father's blood just as I've got mine. Only difference is, neither of you would come at me like men, but you'd hire others to do your dirty work. Or you'd keep trying to ambush me and my friends."

The two men leaned forward, eyes flickering to their guns still lying in the dust at their feet.

"If you gun us down," the taller brother said, "our cowboys will make sure that none of you leave this ranch yard alive."

"Hell," the other brother said, "that Chinaman son of

180

a bitch is a dead man anyway. We ain't going to let him go."

Dustin looked out to see the AC cowboys emerging from the outbuildings. Confused, they stopped and stared at Alonzo Cobb lying face to the sun with his neck pumping blood. Dustin knew that if he shot these two young killers, Jessie and Ki would die with him in a hail of bullets.

"Jessie," he said, "turn the wagon around and git!"

"No!"

"Ki, damn you, make her do it!"

Ki sized up the situation. He knew what had to happen. Dustin was not going to allow these brothers to come after him. He was not going to make the same mistake as his father.

Ki took the lines from Jessie's hands, saying, "It's too late. We *have* to go."

A protest formed on Jessie's lips and tears filled her eyes. She clenched her fists tightly together and said to Dustin, "Good-bye."

"Prettiest woman in Texas," Dustin said, swaying on his feet and grinning like a lovesick fool.

Ki sawed on the lines and turned the team around, heading toward Laredo. The AC cowboys wanted to block their exit but their ranks broke and Ki made the horses run.

Less than a mile out, Jessie and Ki heard the rolling thunder of gunfire.

"He's dead," Jessie whispered. "The Texas Tornado is dead."

"He was trouble, Jessie, and he'd been dead for a long, long time."

Jessie scrubbed hot tears from her eyes and wanted to

fiercely argue that point. After all, she'd grown to know and love Dustin Gamble. But she held her tongue and stared straight ahead because, as much as she hated to admit it, Ki was right.

Watch for

LONE STAR AND THE TEMPERANCE ARMY

149th in the exciting LONE STAR series
from Jove

Coming in January!

If you would like to read more of the very best, most exciting, adventurous, action-packed Westerns being published today, you'll want to subscribe to True Value's Western Home Subscription Service.

Each month the editors of True Value will select the 6 very best Westerns from America's leading publishers for special readers like you. You'll be able to preview these new titles as soon as they are published, *FREE* for ten days with no obligation!

TWO FREE BOOKS

When you subscribe, we'll send you your first month's shipment of the newest and best 6 Westerns for you to preview. With your first shipment, two of these books will be yours as our introductory gift to you absolutely *FREE* (a $7.00 value), regardless of what you decide to do. If you like them, as much as we think you will, keep all six books but pay for just 4 at the low subscriber rate of just $2.75 each. If you decide to return them, keep 2 of the titles as our gift. No obligation.

Special Subscriber Savings

When you become a True Value subscriber you'll save money several ways. First, all regular monthly selections will be billed at the low subscriber price of just $2.75 each. That's at least a savings of $4.50 each month below the publishers price. Second, there is never any shipping, handling or other hidden charges—*Free home delivery*. What's more there is no minimum number of books you must buy, you may return any selection for full credit and you can cancel your subscription at any time. A TRUE VALUE!